YESTERDAY NEVER DIES

YESTERDAY NEVER DIES

DIE AGAIN TO SAVE THE WORLD™ BOOK THREE

RAMY VANCE

MICHAEL ANDERLE

THE YESTERDAY NEVER DIES TEAM

Thanks to our Beta Reader
Rachel Beckford

Thanks to the JIT Readers

Dorothy Lloyd
Jackey Hankard-Brodie
Veronica Stephan-Miller
Deb Mader
Zacc Pelter
Debi Sateren
Paul Westman

If I've missed anyone, please let me know!

Editor
The Skyhunter Editing Team

LMBPN Publishing
PMB 196, 2540 South Maryland Pkwy
Las Vegas, NV 89109

Version 1.00, July 2021
ISBN (ebook) 978-1-64971-932-4
ISBN (paperback) 978-1-64971-933-1

For my mom ... who let me 'RePeat' so many of my mistakes

—Ramy Vance

*To Family, Friends and
Those Who Love
to Read.
May We All Enjoy Grace
to Live the Life We Are
Called.*

— Michael

Rueben Peet trudged through the bowels of the tanker, not a soul in sight, the silent halls heavy with the weight of desolation.

All around him were drab gray walls, dotted only by the occasional bulletin board or notice dated some half a decade ago. The floors, although finished to a shine, carried an effervescent layer of dirt that no mop job, no matter how assiduous, could ever save. Along the walls sat thick metal machinery, weighted by the ton, that seemed imported from the industrial era. Now they pivoted, swiveled, spun, steamed, and spat like an Old West railcar springing to life.

It was a cold and awful place, and he needed to find the command center and get on with the mission before the foreign Special Ops team reached it.

He ran his gloved finger over a laminated floor plan tacked to the wall. According to the map and a little bit of deductive logic, the tanker's command center should be one of two rooms at the end of a hallway upstairs. It wasn't clear which one. He would have to figure that out for himself.

The rooms were up three flights of stairs, cold metal steps with creaky handrails drilled into the wall. Rueben slowly plodded up them. He wore a full hazmat suit, and the thing was heavy, making him slog through the place like an earthbound astronaut with his breath fogging up the plastic face shield. He got up the stairs and down a couple more dismal halls and found two identical metal doors.

He opened the first one and stepped inside. He glanced at all the pipes in the room. Nothing of importance in here. As he was about to leave, a line suddenly burst with a *hiss* and spat hot steam at him.

He dodged to the side and spotted the shutoff valve. After rolling his shoulders and flexing his fingers within the confines of the suit, he approached the small metal wheel, set his gloved palms against its hot curvature, and turned. It was stuck. There was a fire extinguisher on the wall, so he grabbed it and crashed it down upon the wheel to loosen it. Then, grunting with the effort, he turned the wheel. The valve *squealed* shut, silencing the leak in the pipe. He hoped the Spec Ops team hadn't heard. It was a big ship, but he wasn't holding his breath.

He shook his head at the offending pipe that had gassed him. "Take that, asshole."

He left the room and turned to the second metal door. Someone had locked it. He jerked the doorknob back and forth hard, trying to force it to release. That didn't work, so he rammed his body against it. It still didn't budge. He bent down to inspect the mechanism. It was a rather cheap one, but the door was strong.

He looked around for something he could use to pick it. He was in luck. A glassed-in bulletin board posted an inspection checklist and offered a pen hanging from a string and paperclip. If he broke the glass, it would provide more sound for his enemies to hear him. Still, he'd already made some noise shutting off that pipe and if they killed him—again—he'd warp back a few minutes and find another way around them.

With a hard pound, he slammed one muscular forearm into the cover and smashed in the glass. Even through his suit, he thought he felt a warm trickle of blood. Had the glass punctured the covering? Aki would fuss at him for that. She hated it when he did what she called "superhero stunts."

She'd chide him, "Just because you're immortal doesn't mean you can be reckless."

Umm…yes, it did.

He gave his arm a cursory glance and didn't see a tear in his suit. That didn't mean it wasn't there. What did it matter though? His gear wasn't measuring any toxic or radioactive materials on the tanker. Buzz and Aki could be so overly protective at times.

With the glass shattered, he reached inside, ripped the pen off the wall, and pulled off the paperclip. In less than a minute, Rueben picked the lock on the metal door and eased it open.

This was it. He'd found it. The tanker's command center. His last stop before he scuttled the vessel.

He mused that now in his forties, he could kick ass like he never could in his twenties. Wasn't it supposed to be the other way around?

The command center was a small, cluttered, and dank room. It contained dark furniture and a disorganized console full of unusual technology—one part steampunk, the other part hacker.

He sat in the tattered leather chair and gingerly moved a

paper coffee cup, half-full of solidified contents. He checked out the console. Sadly, he'd been enough of a tech nerd when he was younger that he knew of these operating systems. Now at the age of forty-five, Rueben had forgotten a lot of that stuff.

Not forgotten. Replaced it with more useful knowledge, like how to fight.

After a few minor missteps, he booted up the machines and pulled up all the files he could find.

Everything about the tanker seemed off. Seemingly unmanned and traveling full-steam toward the coast of New York, it had warranted the attention of Rueben's team. His team included only three people: him, his team leader and wife Aki, and his tech specialist best bud Buzz.

Their mission was to investigate and disable the tanker before it could reach the mainland. Rueben had been surprised to find it empty. He was even more surprised by the Spec Ops team that had reached it at the same time as him.

It hadn't been easy getting in here. Truth be told, he'd died six times to get in, not that he'd ever admit it to his team. Those foreign agents filtering through the tanker were packing some heat. Definitely Special Forces, but from what country, he couldn't tell. He'd finally learned to avoid them altogether. It had taken a lot of stealth.

He sighed when he thought about facing off against them again on his way off the tanker. He'd probably have to die another six times. Argh. You'd think after close to four thousand deaths he'd be used to it by now, but somehow dying never got easier.

Guess that's the way we're hard-wired, he thought as he started copying all the computer files for Buzz to analyze.

He hooked up his phone to the computer and started

transferring the files. Then he pulled up both Buzz and Aki on video chat on his phone.

He told them, "Transferring the files now. There was no one in the command center."

Buzz didn't look at all surprised, but that could have been the plastic surgery he'd had ten years ago. "Can you transfer them any faster?"

Rueben shook his head. "This computer system is outdated."

"Damn. Well, I'm combing through the files as they come. I'll see what I can find."

Rueben's phone connection jumped in and out, and Aki's question was jumbled up and scrambled. He finally made it out. "Are you doing okay?"

Buzz cut her off. "Okay, I just found something. I don't think this is about the tanker at all. This is incredible. I wish I could talk with the person who designed this—"

"Stay focused," Rueben said. "We're running out of time. I need to stop this tanker before it reaches the mainland."

Buzz cleared his throat. "I know. I know. You're right." On the phone screen, he squinted at his laptop. "Other countries would die for the data in these files."

"Explains the Special Ops team I ran up against."

"Are you sure you're okay?" Aki asked.

"Sure. Chicks dig scars, right Aki babe?"

Her connection was stronger now, and she came in loud and clear. "Oh, absolutely, Rueben. I would have never gotten with you if it wasn't for the scars. Totally sealed the deal." She looked off-screen and snapped her fingers. "Hey, don't touch that." She popped off-screen for a second and came back breathless, smoothing her silky dark hair into place.

Rueben smiled. Even after all these years, she still made his heart race. Now, there were three. "What's the little rug rat up to now?"

She sighed and rolled her dark eyes. "You know, getting into everything as usual… Hey, I said 'no.'" She snapped again and disappeared, then returned. "Mama needs wine."

Buzz chimed in and clapped his hands. "Can we focus, people? I've never seen anything like this before. Are you in position to destroy the computer and—"

Rueben cut him off. "I got it, Buzz. I'll follow the plan and blah, blah, blah."

Buzz's eyes flashed. "Hey, if this is all a big joke to you—"

Rueben sighed. "It's not a big joke. Otherwise, I wouldn't be here. But it's not as serious as you think. If the whole op goes belly up, eh, whatever. I just kill myself and reset. We've got nothing to lose here."

Aki sighed. "There you go again with your superhero stunts."

Buzz frowned. "As much as I enjoy killing you, and I do…"

Rueben rolled his eyes. Buzz did and had recently hit pay dirt with his latest book, *Lethal*. Not that Buzz needed any more money. It was a novel about a mad scientist who killed people in his basement and meticulously wrote down all the medical facts on how they died. A movie studio optioned the novel and turned it into a blockbuster Hollywood hit that had become a staple in the Halloween horror circuit.

Buzz straightened and suddenly turned solemn. "Seriously though, I've told you once, I'll tell you a million times…you warp back when you die, but there are possible abnormalities that may reset with you. There's a lot we don't know about your powers."

The two of them ganging up on him about his recklessness irritated him. It was his power, after all. "In the three thousand seven hundred and eighty-nine deaths I've had, has any weird abnormality ever happened?"

"No. It's been three thousand seven hundred and eighty-three, by the way. Unless... Aki!" Buzz called. "I win the bet. He died six times already. You owe me pizza."

"Pizza? You guys betting on my deaths again?"

"Yep. I bet her you couldn't complete this mission without five deaths, minimum. She said three."

"Thanks for betting on me, babe," Rueben said. "Next time let me know, and I'll be sure to win it for you." Rueben chuckled. "And as for the probability of this anomaly thingy happening when I warp, it's what? One in seven million?"

Buzz searched upward. "Probably more like seven billion."

"Exactly. So what's the problem, then?"

Buzz looked at him sternly. "People win the lottery all the time, Rueben. This is one lottery we don't want to win."

Rueben didn't respond to that. Instead, he inspected the computer screen. The file transfer was almost finished. "So what do you think? Are the Russians or the Chinese behind this stunt?"

Buzz pursed his lips. "Not sure yet."

Rueben nodded. Buzz would figure it out. He always did.

The file transfer completed, and Rueben severed the link to Buzz.

Rueben stood. "Well, I'm off to scuttle the ship."

"You've got the bombs, right?" Aki asked.

"Sure." Rueben unshouldered his tactical backpack. It contained small but concentrated explosives that would destroy the tanker if placed strategically. He'd already planted a few of them as he'd made his way here. Now it was time for the rest. He dusted off a good place to put one in the command room and primed it. That's when he noticed it.

It was a shiny metal box, resting amid the clutter in front of him. It seemed out of place. On it was etched a single word in a flowing font: *Nunez*.

Hmm. What was in the metal box and why was it in this abandoned tanker? Maybe the foreign agents weren't after the computer files but this box instead.

He looked at Aki and Buzz on his phone. He held up the box. "You guys see this?"

They both nodded.

"I wonder what's inside."

Aki jumped in. "Rueben, just get out of there. Come back to me, okay."

Buzz disagreed. "I think you should open it."

Rueben agreed. "Relax, Aki. I'll come back to you. There's nothing in this box that could be any more dangerous than...*Lethal*."

He threw the jibe at Buzz, who sighed and leaned back in his chair with a disapproving look. "Come on, now. Don't hate on *Lethal*. It grossed twenty million at the box office on opening weekend."

Rueben shook his head, then reassured Aki, "It's okay. If I die, I'll just reset." He set the box on the counter and slowly opened it. He stared at the contents. "Holy fuck. What is this?"

CHAPTER ONE

<u>Monday, May 22, 10:03 p.m.</u>

Summit, New York, New York—Earth-A

Firefighters worked to quash the flames flickering outside the United Nations building while medics and police officers poured through the lingering smoke, tending to the wounded. Although it was night, countless flashing lights and portable halogen lamps lit up the place as bright as day. Amid the chaos, reporters swarmed around with microphones and cameras, searching for stories.

The story they wouldn't receive was that Rueben Peet and his friends had prevented a global nuclear war. Although they'd avoided the worst-case scenario, several people had died—all because Rueben hadn't died and warped back in time to save them all.

He hadn't had a choice. The perpetrator was a Repeater like him. Had he not succeeded in disabling his warping powers, it was possible that no amount of repeats could've prevented World War III.

At least that's over now, he would have thought, had his head not still been reeling from the woman's voice he'd heard and her face he'd seen in the artificial brightness of the parking lot.

Rueben rubbed his temple, worried he might've gotten hit in the head sometime in all the action. "Mom? Mom, is that…you?"

The blonde-haired reporter smiled weakly at him, the harsh illumination highlighting the bags under her eyes. She started to reach out toward him and stopped.

A warm hand gripped Rueben's arm, and he turned to see Aki's dark eyes filled with concern.

"It's okay," Rueben said softly and realized that it was far from okay. He whipped his head back to the mother he hadn't seen in fifteen years, his face wrinkled with confusion.

Buzz caught up with him. "Holy shit, buddy. Isn't that your mom?"

Aki gasped and removed her hand from Rueben's arm. "Your mom?"

Rueben was vaguely aware of more footsteps behind him, and he turned to see his childhood friend Martha and Zach the police intern. One glance at Martha's face revealed that she had seen his mother too. Of all his friends, only Martha had ever known his mom.

"Carolyn," Martha said and, after clearing her throat, she turned to Buzz, Aki, and Zach. "Guys, let's um, give these two some space?"

Zach and Aki nodded understandingly and started to walk away, but Buzz lingered, not catching her point. Martha flashed Rueben a supportive glance, gripped Buzz by the wrist, and tugged him after her.

Now it was only Rueben and Carolyn and a thin waft of smoke that had blown between them like a veil so that they could barely see each other's features for a moment. Then it dissipated, and Rueben realized he should say something.

"Where…"

"Oh, Rueben." Carolyn rushed forward and wrapped her arms around him. "You're okay. You're okay."

So many conflicting emotions rushed through Rueben that he couldn't begin to pin them down. Next came the flood of memories of her when he grew up: her helping him tie his shoelaces for the first time, her backing away from the oven with a tray of fresh-baked cookies in her mitt, her stepping into the crowd and leaving him…

He was a certifiable hero. He didn't need to deal with this right now.

Suddenly he pushed her back from him and twisted out of her embrace.

"Rueben…"

"Mom…" He figured he ought to apologize, but then some cameras flashed off to the side of him again, and he turned and finally saw the point of the reporters' interest.

Fifteen yards away from them, a buff man wearing an open leather jacket was posing with one arm flexed. Dirt and ash spotted his chiseled jaw, strong forehead, and spiked-up hair, and he had makeshift tourniquets tied around his arm and leg. "Welcome to the gun show," he was telling the microphone-toting reporters as several of the most attractive women Rueben had ever seen cooed and shouldered up to the man and rubbed his sore muscles.

Well, they weren't exactly women, Rueben knew, but

robots named Binnie that his best friend Buzz had created. They were so lifelike that they could pass as human though, and they had played a crucial part in defending the U.N. building as they'd shot down the drones attacking the summit.

"Fucking Mike Fury," Rueben muttered.

"Excuse me?" Carolyn said.

"Nothing." Rueben rested a hand on his mother's shoulder and was about to apologize for his actions when he realized she was blinking from the most recent barrage of camera flashes.

"Thanks," Mike was saying, "for all the kind words, but the real hero is over there." He was pointing at Rueben.

Are you kidding me...

With his hand still on his mother's shoulder, he guided her away from the crowd of reporters. They passed through the smoke of a smoldering pile of debris and nodded at a crew of firefighters as they worked to extinguish a neighboring blaze in the parking lot.

When he was sure that they'd momentarily lost the reporters, Rueben stopped and confronted his mother again. He swallowed. There were too many questions to ask. When his eyes fell to his mother's reporter's attire, the words spilled out of his mouth. "You left Dad and me to be a reporter? In the same city as us..."

His mother winced and shook her head. "Not a reporter." She tilted her chin down and eyed the mic clipped to her blazer.

"Then what..." He let his words trail off as he caught sight of her face and realized she had just as many thoughts and emotions swirling through her head.

She suddenly reached out and touched his wrist. "I'm

dressed like this because I was trying to stop him. Or at least help the wounded if I couldn't." She sighed, her shoulders rising and falling as if she bore a great burden.

"Him?" Rueben's voice tightened. "Are you talking about Pete?" Of course, she had to be. Pete, the madman who had attacked the summit was the future version of himself from another universe. And Carolyn was his mom… Wait, was she both of their moms?

If Rueben thought his head hurt earlier, now it felt like it was clamped in a vice and lit on flames from the inside.

Carolyn studied Rueben's face. "Pete?" Before she could say anything else, camera flashes approached them through the smoky parking lot.

"Sir! Sir, do you have a comment on what happened today?"

Rueben grabbed Carolyn's wrist, and they made off in the opposite direction. They needed to get out of there. They needed to get somewhere safe. First, he needed to regroup with his friends.

A few minutes later, Rueben stood with Aki and Martha next to a bench on the sidewalk not far from the U.N. building.

"Where's Zach?" Rueben asked.

Martha rolled her eyes. "He and Buzz were posing with Mike and the Binnies. Knowing him, he'll probably wind up taking one of those reporters home."

Aki screwed up her face. "Who? Buzz?"

"Zach," Martha said, and the two of them stifled laughs.

"Buzz?" Carolyn said.

Rueben swallowed. It was still confusing having his mom here. "My college roommate from Columbia."

Carolyn smiled. "I know. He seems like a good friend. What I meant was, where is he?"

She knew? Shit. Had his mom been keeping tabs on him after she'd abandoned him? Did she know about his almost marriage to his ex-fiancée Rachel and how bad his relationship was with his father?

Rueben shook his head to clear it. "Yeah. Buzz is a good friend." What was his mom's angle? Ugh. He needed answers.

Martha carefully eyed Rueben and Carolyn. "Buzz said to leave him. You know how he is with the spotlight. Probably trying to get an interview."

Rueben nodded and glanced down the street lamp-lit sidewalk, cursing to himself when he caught sight of a figure with a bulky camera resting on his shoulder.

"There they are," the cameraman shouted from a block away, pointing in their direction.

Martha sighed irritably and pulled out her cell phone. "These guys don't give up. I would call for police backup to give us a ride out, but they're needed here." She gestured at the devastation back at the U.N. building.

Aki caught her riff. "Don't worry. I already have a car coming for us."

Rueben scratched his head. "You think an Uber is going to be able to get through all the roadblocks around here?"

"It's a company car." Aki had a glint in her eye. That meant someone from the CIA was on the way to whisk them away, probably in an armored SUV or limo. Working for the agency had its perks.

Rueben didn't know if his mom knew he worked for the CIA or not. She shouldn't, but there was so much he didn't know about her. Plus the sudden way she'd appeared in his life now. To say it was a bit fishy would be an understatement. She was caught up in this Pete business somehow.

He noticed that she kept glancing over her shoulders, her eyes flitting to the shadows of alleys and awning-covered storefronts. Although Pete had escaped earlier, Rueben had hobbled him with the help of his friends. Once immortal, now Pete had only one life to live. Was Carolyn worried about Pete coming after them? The man would be no match for Rueben.

Regardless, Rueben let his eyes glance to the shadows on the street as Aki abruptly raised a hand. Headlights blinked at them, and a limo pulled up alongside them on the curb.

"Where are we going to go?" Martha asked.

Rueben noticed his mother biting her lip and he turned to her questioningly.

She scratched behind her head. "These reporters. They have your faces on camera. It's only a matter of time before they track down your addresses."

"Buzz's mansion," Aki said, and they all turned to her. "GPS doesn't take you there. I'm good with directions, but I would never have found it without Rueben's instructions."

Martha agreed. "Rosa probably wouldn't let any reporters near the front door even if they could find the place."

The limo stopped beside them, and the driver's window rolled down. "Mr. Peet, Ms. Yamashiro, I'm here to pick you up. My instructions are to take you anywhere you'd like to go."

Martha's mouth dropped. "Nice ride."

Aki gave her a sly smile and Rueben, Aki, Martha, and Carolyn all piled into the limo. Martha gushed over every detail—the interior, the complimentary champagne, and everything else in between.

Rueben resisted the urge. He was impressed with the luxury accommodations, but he was too wrapped up in his family problems to think about it all: why his mother was back, why she'd left in the first place, and what she knew about Pete.

He glanced over at Aki and saw that she had her eyes on her phone screen, getting caught up on everything she'd missed at the agency while they'd been trying to thwart Pete's plan. "Shit. Sven wants a full report by the end of the week."

"Shit," Rueben agreed, and his mom gave him a questioning look. He opened his mouth, but what was he supposed to say? No one outside of his friends knew he worked at the CIA.

Luckily, Martha saw what was going on and touched Carolyn on the shoulder. They started talking softly. A few moments later, there was a loud *pop* and a bubbling bottle of champagne in Martha's hands. Rueben didn't drink any though. Aside from giving the driver directions to Buzz's place, Rueben rested his head back against the seat. He was so tired of everything. Tired of saving the world. Tired of surprises. Just tired.

***

Finally, the limo pulled into the circular drive in front of Buzz's mansion. Having been driving here for years, Rueben hadn't realized how hard it was to get here without GPS, but he could now understand what his friends had been saying. They thanked the driver and stepped out of the car.

In the dark, it was difficult to see the details of the drive—the lilacs and the birdbath—but Martha filled Carolyn in as the car drove away. "It's gorgeous here in the daytime. The gardens, the hedges, the fountains. You'll love it. He has a manicured hedge maze and an observation deck, and God only knows what else."

They all laughed, and Rueben replied, "Yeah, I'm with you on the 'God only knows what else' thing."

Carolyn craned her neck and stared at the high arched columns and multiple levels. "Beautiful."

Rueben gestured toward the front door. "Shall we?"

They approached the door, and without Buzz around, no one wanted to press the doorbell and wake Rosa at this hour. Rueben had the guest code to the smart lock, so they quietly let themselves in. As many times as Rueben had been here, the entrance still took his breath away.

Carolyn gasped when they walked in. The high vaulted ceilings with the African wildlife fresco and winding double staircases in the foyer made it hard not to be impressed.

They all stood in the foyer, and for the first time all night, it was quiet.

Then Carolyn pulled Rueben aside. "We need to talk. You and me. I think we're all in grave danger."

CHAPTER TWO

<u>**Monday, May 22, 11:22 p.m.**</u>

Rueben stared at his mom. Martha and Aki soon took the hint and meandered off through the mansion. In the warm lighting of Buzz's foyer, Carolyn was as pretty as he remembered from his childhood, but she had lost that spark that had made her magnetic, irresistible, and the embodiment of "home." She was simply a woman now and a weary one at that.

Carolyn dug her reporter's disguise pumps deep into the plush white rug beneath her. She nodded approvingly. "Buzz has done well for himself."

Standing across from her, Rueben shrugged. "How is that related to how we're in grave danger?"

Carolyn dropped her gaze embarrassedly. "How about we catch up a bit first?"

Her mysterious demeanor bothered him. Being raised mostly by Marshall, Rueben was never that good at expressing feelings. He had long ago learned to repress them,

10

and they were more likely to come out with sarcasm and passive aggression.

Her blue eyes clouded with guilt as if she knew what he was thinking. "Tell me, what are you up to these days?"

"You don't know? I work for the government." Uneasy emotions tugged at his chest. Off to the side of him, he spotted a crystal decanter filled with Scotch sitting on the living room bar. Maybe some alcohol would help. It helped Buzz. "Drink?" He held up a crystal decanter filled with Scotch.

"I'd love one."

He poured two glasses, and the gentle *splash* of liquid was the only sound in the room.

There was so much to say, and he didn't know where to start. Why was she hedging? What did she know about Pete? Ugh, he really didn't want to get into all of his mother issues right now. On top of which, his mother issues were part of his father issues, and those were a whole different species.

Wow, he was fucked up.

Maybe his time warp power wasn't a genetic anomaly but some kind of trauma response to his dysfunctional family life.

Hah. He scoffed and handed her one of the glasses. Then they took seats on two couches opposite each other, and both drank slowly. He gave her another once-over, then leaned back into the leather of the sofa. Crossing his legs, he balanced the Scotch glass on his knee, tapping his fingers against it. "Um…" *Fuck it,* he thought. Screw catching up and this grave danger they were facing. "Why did you leave?"

She gripped the glass in her hand, and her voice turned soft. "That's a very complicated question."

"One that you no doubt came here intending to answer. Right?" Surely she hadn't expected to appear in his life without explaining her past actions. He knew he was too hard on her. Maybe some of Marshall's assholeness was rubbing off on him.

She smiled fondly. "You're smart. Of course, you've always been. That's no surprise." She sighed. "You deserve an explanation. Leaving was never what I wanted. God, it was the last thing I wanted to do. It killed me, and that's the truth."

Her glistening tears melted Rueben's anger a little, but his voice came out with more force than he expected. "Then why?"

"There's more going on than you know. Your universe is younger than the others—"

Rueben cut her off. "You're not answering my question."

She made a face, that maternal look he remembered from his early childhood that meant he had pushed her buttons too hard. "It was because of him…Thorne."

Rueben's eyes widened. "Thorne? The man who attacked my school bus when I was in the fifth grade?"

She nodded, and Rueben let the idea sink in.

His voice cracked with emotion as he remembered. "That was the day you left. I *knew* you were there. I saw you in the crowd. I yelled for you."

Tears flowed down her cheeks. "I know. Walking away from you was difficult. Afterward, I nearly killed myself so I could go back in time and stay."

Rueben's throat constricted and his gut clenched. "You. You're a…" He couldn't say the word.

"Repeater?" Carolyn said.

Rueben swallowed.

"I am."

Realizing he'd been holding his breath, Rueben drew in a long deep breath. The room seemed to be cracking as the reckoning of his life shattered in one messy blast. "You're a Repeater? Like me?"

She nodded.

"Then why didn't you come back to me?"

Carolyn shook her head sadly. "I couldn't."

Rueben started to feel light-headed and numb, and he sucked in a couple more long deep breaths. "Wait, was Thorne a Repeater too?"

His mother winced at Thorne's name. "No. But he wanted to be, more than anything. That's what he wanted from me. That's why…"

Rueben's mouth dropped in shock. The biggest illusion of his entire childhood kept blowing up right in front of him. "Thorne was holding us hostage to get to you?"

"Thorne wasn't a Repeater, but he has this ability that… Well, you know the homeless guy in this city who knows more than he should?"

Rueben nodded uneasily.

"His name is Organic Jim…and don't ask. It's what he wants people to call him. He and Thorne have this ability to see multiple timelines all at once. They can't Repeat, but they can remember things that didn't happen, and both of them have been driven crazy by it. With Organic Jim, he's mostly harmless. But Thorne… Well, Thorne did what he did."

"Used me to get to you."

She nodded. "When I was about your age—this was before I had you—I was admitted to the psychiatric ward because I said some things about my power to a friend. Well, they shared my secret, and it was only a matter of time before the guys with the white coats came for me. Psych ward."

Rueben nodded. He remembered when he'd first found

out about his powers and had wanted someone to turn to that he could trust.

"Once I got out, a reporter for an alt science newspaper heard about it and wanted to interview me. After everything I'd been through, I didn't want to talk about it. He was persistent so I did one interview and developed a following I never wanted. That was where Thorne came in."

"He was a news writer?"

That made sense. Tabloid writers would do anything to get their hands on woo-woo stories, complicated conspiracies, and juicy controversies.

She shook her head. "No. He subscribed to that newspaper I mentioned. Once Thorne read my interview, he tracked down my address and started stalking me for years. He wanted my power and thought I could give it to him."

"And Dad knew you had a stalker?"

She nodded. "I think that was part of the reason why he joined the force."

Rueben stared at her in disbelief. Marshall had known she was a Repeater all these years and hadn't told him? He suddenly recalled how his dad had started to tell him something at Buzz's bar when they were preparing for the summit attack. Then they had gotten into a fight and never finished the conversation. "Dad became a cop because you had a stalker?"

"Yeah. Believe it or not, he was going to be a computer engineer."

"I'm sorry, Marshall Peet was going to be a computer engineer?"

"That's what he went to college for."

Rueben didn't know his father had gone to college. He'd never said anything about it, ever. After all the grief Marshall had given him about sitting around on his ass playing with circuit boards…

Carolyn continued, "As soon as he got into the computer science field, Marshall hated it. He sat in a cubicle day after day, and it drained the life out of him. Then one day when I was pregnant, he was at work, and Thorne broke into the house and threatened me with a gun. He held me hostage for hours. I finally managed to get away and called the cops. They didn't really do anything, just took some reports and that was it. I was so traumatized that I lost the baby."

"You had a miscarriage?" He was supposed to have had a sibling?

She nodded. It took a few moments for her to compose herself and continue. "Your father was so broken up about it. He saw it as the government had failed us. That we couldn't trust them to find the psychopath that had ruined our lives. He became convinced he could do better, so he decided to become a cop."

Rueben's mouth dropped. "I never knew any of this"

"Of course you didn't. Who would have told you? Marshall?"

"You have a point there."

"Thorne was convinced that I could give him my power somehow. No matter how many restraining orders, no matter how many times he got thrown in jail, no matter how many times I tried to explain to him that I couldn't, he'd always come back looking for us. The rest of the cops thought he was looney and didn't take him seriously as a threat to my family or me."

The truth of Rueben's life began to dawn on him in layers, and he suddenly felt utterly drained. "So the hostage situation, he was using me to get to you…"

"He held you hostage because he believed that I would finally give him my power."

Rueben mused. "Like a vampire."

"Something like that. Except it doesn't work that way. I don't know how it works except I die, and I warp back in time anywhere from a few seconds to about three days."

With a tired groan, Rueben leaned back into the couch and sank deeper into the luxuriously soft leather.

She continued, "You wouldn't believe how many times I died trying to save you from Thorne—and not only on that bus."

He shook his head. "This is crazy. I know I was only a kid at the time but how did I not know any of this was going on? You said yourself that I was smart."

"You were. It wasn't easy. Your father and I decided early on that we didn't want you to know about my power to protect you. We didn't want my problem to be your problem.

"We knew there was a chance you had the gene too—if that's what it was that caused the ability—but God in heaven, we weren't going to try to find out. So we kept it from you and all of the secrets that went with it. I guess they got more and more complicated over the years. Maybe we should have told you, but when you're a parent, you make the best decision you can and hope it's the right one."

Rueben's head was hurting. He rose and grabbed his glass. "You want another drink?"

She handed him her empty glass. He poured the drinks and handed hers to her. She continued as he sat. "You know I died almost five hundred times trying to protect you from him."

That shouldn't have surprised him after all he had been through recently, but it did.

"You don't know how many different times I warped back in time to prevent Thorne from getting you before the bus incident. One time he kidnapped you from school. Another time it was while you were getting ice cream from the ice cream truck in front of our house."

His head spun with the new information. Or was it the booze?

She continued. "The repeated exertions and always looking over my shoulder...it drained me completely. It killed your father to have to see me that way. And Thorne just wouldn't leave us alone.

"By the time he attacked the bus, I was at my wit's end. It was far from the best scenario, but...I was ready for it to be over. Not that it would ever be over. If Thorne ever stopped, another threat would come up sooner or later. Someone else like Thorne. Or maybe government scientists. As long as I was around, you and Marshall were in danger."

Carolyn drew in a breath. "But back to the bus incident. The last twenty times, I was training your dad how to save the kids on the bus. I kept having to die and go back and relive it again."

That explained why Carolyn had been there that day after the bus had stopped. "You were there, helping Marshall. Showing him what worked and what didn't."

She nodded. "The last time I died, I realized the only way to be free of Thorne would be to kill him." Carolyn steeled herself. "After he was dead, and you were safe, I thought..." Her eyes welled up, and she tried again. "I thought the best thing would be to leave."

She began to sob, and after a few moments, Rueben got up and sat next to her. He wrapped his arm around her. The distance between them still felt awkward, but for the first time, he was starting to understand her and her difficult decision. If he'd been in her position, he didn't know that he would have done things any differently. Years of confusion and frustration that had begun to build to anger started to melt away like a glacier.

Eventually, she calmed and sighed. "It took too many years before I realized I had made the wrong choice. I always thought you and your father would make it together. He's a strong man, a good man. I knew he would take care of you and keep you safe."

"Well, he kind of went crazy after you left. He's, he's broken."

"I know. It was a mistake." She paused. "Tell me, does he get his hash browns?"

Rueben laughed hard, partly from the tension release, partly because he was a little buzzed, but mainly because after all these years, she'd remembered. "Marshall Peet and breakfast."

She rolled her eyes. "He always has to have his breakfast food just right, or the man loses his mind."

Rueben chuckled. "Hash browns. Gotta have the hash browns."

She rubbed her forehead. "The hash browns. God forbid if I ever got the frozen ones. I always had to make them from scratch."

"I remember that. Sorry, I cheap out and get the frozen ones."

"Well, you should. It's good for him not to be so spoiled."

A silence passed between them, and finally, Rueben broke it. "Have you seen him yet? Aside from when he happened to see you at the Exit Bar, I mean."

She shook her head. "Not yet. He tried to run after me, but

I wasn't ready to confront him yet." She touched his shoulder, then engulfed him in a hug. Rueben was shocked at the emotions that came up in him. Then they were both crying. She released him and wiped her eyes.

Rueben couldn't believe what was happening. The story, her being a Repeater. It was all so unbelievable, but he knew it was true. He wanted to sink into it all, accept it, but he'd died too many times to do that. There were so many questions.

Why hadn't he known any of this about Marshall being in computer science?

Why hadn't he heard about Thorne? God, what had Marshall mentally gone through after shooting Thorne the day of the bus incident? Had it been in self-defense or had it been a cold-blooded killing? Either way, it could help to explain some of Marshall's behavior after Carolyn left. He'd have to talk with Marshall soon to clear the air between them.

Rueben rubbed his head. After his mom had left, he'd have thought Marshall would've let something slip. There was so much his parents had kept him in the dark about.

All of that could wait.

"The danger you mentioned," Rueben said. "And Pete. He said he's from a parallel universe. So how do you know about him—"

"There is something else I need to tell you," Carolyn said softly.

What other life-changing revelation could Carolyn possibly make? Rueben steeled himself by trying to make a joke of it. "Is this the part where you tell me you're not from this world either?"

Carolyn pursed her lips.

Rueben's gut sank. "Wait. So you...you're not from this

universe? Oh, God. Oh God, no. That's how you know about him?"

She nodded and dropped her head to her knees for a few moments before straightening to face him. A fresh batch of tears stained her cheeks. "I'm from the same parallel Earth as him. I'm his mother. I've been trying to run from Pete, and this isn't the first world I've gone to try to escape him." She paused before turning to him with a grave look on her face.

"Wait," Rueben said. "You look like you're the same age as Marshall and Pete. If you're Pete's mother, you should be like sixty years old…" His world was spinning. There was so much that didn't make sense.

"Listen, Rueben. There's more going on here than you know. I promise I'll explain everything—including my age and what happened to the Carolyn on this Earth—but now he's found this world. That means a very dark future is coming. A future that I hoped to spare this universe from."

CHAPTER THREE

<u>Monday, May 22, 11:20 p.m.</u>

These people had some fucked up family issues.

That thought was on Martha's mind as she and Aki picked their way through Buzz's mansion. She could only imagine the conversation Rueben and Carolyn must be having right now. Had they made up? Were they shouting at each other? Why had Carolyn come back? She must have had a good reason. Surely she hadn't known how hard her leaving would have been on Rueben and Marshall for all these years.

Martha had tried her best to put Rueben and Carolyn at ease together, but the effort had made her feel like some kind of referee. Especially after that limo ride. Since Rueben had looked like he wanted to be left alone so he could rest, she'd mostly blabbered to Carolyn about mundane topics to pass the time until they had arrived here. Now, Martha felt like another drink, not that the CIA champagne hadn't been good. Oh, the CIA and their agents...

Speaking of agents...Aki. The woman intimidated her, and not many people daunted Martha. She was a cop in NYC for crying out loud, and she could handle herself well, especially in a department dominated by men. So what was it with Aki?

Aki was nice enough, but Martha always felt like the bottom-rung street cop around her. Plus, she had Rueben's attention big time. She worried that he was falling too hard and too fast for her, and Aki would break his heart. Martha knew Rueben, and she knew how hard he'd taken his breakup with his fiancée Rachel. Of course, Rueben was a much tougher guy these days. He'd saved the world not once but twice in the past few months.

Regardless, she'd keep an eye on Aki.

"Hey," Aki said. "What's a girl got to do to find a drink in this place?"

The two of them were meandering down a hallway. Martha found a staircase at the end. Neither she nor Aki had ever been here without Buzz, but she knew the genius loved his liquor. "I don't know, but there's gotta be a bar somewhere around here."

They climbed the stairs. Along the way, they found a mini wax museum dedicated to famous scientists, a room devoted to "Pi Day," and a goat.

Martha jumped back two feet when she opened the door to that room. "A goat? Why does Buzz have a goat?"

Aki grimaced as it nibbled at her shirt. "I couldn't tell you, but it's eating my shirt. Shoo, goat, shoo." The goat turned its attention to her shoe. "Hey!"

They were in a narrow room with vinyl flooring like you might find out on a porch deck or veranda. The room smelled fresh and clean and directly ahead of them were tall potted bushes. It was humid.

Aki muttered, "Buzz is so weird."

Choosing to investigate, they closed the door behind them

and stepped toward the bushes. There was a walkway between two of the plants, and they went through it. On the other side, they both gasped. They'd just stepped out into a huge garden conservatory a few stories high that stretched farther than they could see. Overhead lights *hummed* to life since they'd inadvertently tripped a sensor, illuminating lush vegetation below and to the sides of them.

Martha stood slack-jawed. "Oh my God."

Aki stood there with wide eyes.

A vaulted glass ceiling crowned the conservatory. The black night sky was visible beyond the overhead lights hanging by chains from the greenhouse-like framework. On the ground level were plants and flowers and fountains. A warm breath of fresh humid air greeted them as they stepped toward a railing and observed the beauty. A ramp off to the side gradually led to the ground, and the goat scampered past them and down it.

Aki pointed at the lower level. "Look, it's a river."

A stream ran through the whole conservatory, powered by a waterfall fountain—the largest in the garden, but not the only one. They descended the ramp in awe and walked through the greenery. The sound of rushing water was calming, and like hidden treasures, they kept finding benches and more fountains and waterfalls and trees and plants and a gazebo. And there was a...

"It's a monkey," Martha exclaimed as a small monkey swung over their heads on a hanging rope.

Aki ducked as his flying rear came dangerously close to them. "What the hell? First a goat. Now a monkey?"

"Pretty crazy," Martha agreed.

"I'm waiting for a pet tiger to show up any minute around the corner."

"Or an elephant."

"Buzz would have an elephant, wouldn't he?"

"Yeah, just so he could pretend to be an Arabian prince and go around singing *Aladdin* songs."

They both laughed, and when Martha thought they had discovered everything, Aki bent and carefully lifted the biggest tomato Martha had ever seen, careful not to pick it from the vine. "Vegetables?"

The garden was full of luscious tomatoes, onions, and radishes, and what looked like carrot shoots. But the plants were all so brightly colored they looked like they'd come out of a Pixar movie.

Martha's eyes lit up. "He's doing food experiments out here."

Aki nodded. "Maybe that's what the goat and the monkey are for. To test the food."

Martha knelt and grabbed a handful of dirt in a raised garden bed. She let it pass through her hands, soft and inviting. "Do you think there will ever be a time when we stop being shocked by Buzz?"

"I sincerely doubt it."

They soon reached the stream at the bottom. In the middle of the shallow channel was an island, and they crossed a wooden footbridge to get to it. Martha was trying to figure out what materials he'd constructed the island from when Aki noticed its main fixture: the tiki bar.

Aki winked. "I knew we'd find a bar sooner or later."

"What can I get you?" a male voice asked.

Both women jumped as a tuxedo-clad bartender rose from behind the bar. "I'm Webber. May I take your order?"

Aki and Martha looked at each other. This guy worked here, all alone in Buzz's conservatory?

He stared at them, then lifted a glass and polished it with a white rag. His smile remained on his face, unmoving. He didn't apologize for startling them and didn't offer any further conversation.

That was when Martha noticed that while he polished, his hands repeated the same pattern. "Webber, don't take this the wrong way, but are you a robot?"

"Why yes, I am. Now, what can I get you to drink?"

The girls exchanged glances that said *Holy shit!*

Not that they were too surprised. Buzz's entourage of Binnie model robots had been a great help back at defending the summit from Pete's drone attack. They suspected that Rosa, Buzz's maid, was a robot although he'd never confirmed nor denied that. It stood to reason that Buzz had some "male" robots as well. Yeah, by this point, nothing would surprise them about Buzz.

So now the only real question for them in this fantasy garden land was what would they order?

Aki looked at Martha. "What do you think Webber is programmed to make?"

"Considering he's Buzz's creation, he can likely make anything." Martha decided on her classic standby. "I'll have a daiquiri."

Aki cocked her head. "Margarita."

Webber smiled a hollow smile that kind of creeped Martha out. "One daiquiri and one margarita coming right up."

"Thanks, Webber."

Martha sighed as they strolled about the garden paradise, searching for a place to sit and relax. It had been a long day, and they hadn't had a chance to wind down after the chaos of the day when Carolyn had shown up. With a tired grimace, Martha wondered if she'd have to serve as the Peet family referee for much longer or if Rueben and Carolyn had made amends.

She and Aki found a wrought-iron bistro table near one of the fountains and took a few photos. Once they finished with the photos, Webber came out with their drinks, and they sat and sipped them.

Martha glanced over her drink at Aki. Maybe she was too hard on the woman. She'd seemed all right as they had found their way through the mansion to this place. "You know what?" she said. "I'm glad we got a chance to spend some time together."

Aki smirked. "Me too. To be honest, I didn't know if Rueben had any friends. You seem like you're close to Rueben and his family."

The overly enthusiastic tone bothered Martha, and she wasn't sure whether or not to trust Aki. God, she hated female games. The men she worked with might be crude and vulgar, but they said what they meant and meant what they said.

Aki kept going, "Speaking of Rueben, what can you tell me about his family? I figured his mom was out of the picture."

"Yeah…" Martha knew how Rueben felt about Aki but did Aki feel the same way about him? Or was she passing the time with him until someone better came along? She started slow. "The Peets, they're a complicated family, you know. You have to tread lightly with them all."

Aki leaned closer. "So what's the deal with Carolyn?"

Martha leaned back in her chair and tapped her fingernails against the table. The fountain burbled in the background, and somewhere the goat bleated. Webber swept near them, caught in the same gesture of wiping out the inside of a glass, although there was nothing in either of his hands. She started in on the story. "You know, they used to be a happy little family. Marshall and Carolyn were in love."

"I can't imagine Marshall in love. Or happy, for that matter."

"He was. He was quite the romantic. He'd bring her flowers and leave her little love notes."

"Marshall left love notes?"

"Well, they were Marshall love notes. They weren't terribly creative but sweet in his way. 'Roses are red; violets are blue…' You know, that kind of stuff. He'd hold car doors for her, and they were so cute together."

"What was Carolyn like?"

Martha quieted and stared into the conservatory. Her enduring memory of Carolyn all these years was of her standing in the kitchen, pulling out a pan of freshly baked chocolate chip cookies from the oven. At the time, she and Rueben were kids.

Rueben didn't have much of a sense of humor on his own, so this one time in the kitchen he was trying to figure out what made things funny. So he made up goofy little jokes based on ones he'd read online. He kept a little running list of them. He'd told her his latest joke, and it was funny in his little way, and Carolyn had burst out laughing and nearly dropped the pan.

He'd seemed surprised at her reaction. "Was that really funny, Mom?"

"That was actually funny, Rueben. You did good on that one."

Martha smiled at how tender their little relationship had been. What could have ever made her turn her back on her family and run away? Carolyn had always been such a homey, kind soul.

Martha turned back to Aki. "She laughed a lot and loved to bake cookies. She and Rueben were really close."

"Then what happened?"

"Fifteen years ago. Thorne. The 'incident.' After that, she left. No explanation, nothing. No one has seen or heard from her since. That is, until tonight."

"Damn, that's cold."

"Yep. That's not even the worst of it. Damn near killed Marshall. He fell apart. After the incident, there was a lot of media hype, and he was honored. He got a few cover stories, and someone tried to make a movie out of the whole thing.

"Once that all died down, Marshall just...he just changed. He went from being a sweet little romantic husband to an ogre of a dad. He started drinking all the time, and Rueben kind of became the sane one in the house and took care of him. He was ten years old and started grocery shopping, keeping house, laundry, covering for Marshall when he was drunk.

"Don't get me wrong, Marshall was and is a good man. But he was really mixed up for a long time. He still is in some ways."

"Yeah, I see that."

"One of Marshall's old cop buddies finally got him to see a doctor, and he was diagnosed with depression among other things. They put him on meds, and he started to balance out. Now he's much more manageable. He's still an ogre, but he can get through a day."

"He loved her."

"He did. He really did. And Rueben, he's pretty screwed up about it all, too. He doesn't show it. He never has. I never once saw him cry about his mom. When we were little, I saw him cry about other things. Like, when his turtle Speedy died, and

Rueben cried. He'd picked out the animal at the pet store with his mother. It crushed Rueben after that, but I knew it wasn't about the turtle. It was about her.

"That was the only time I ever heard or saw him express anything about her leaving. He won't talk about her. If someone brings her up, he changes the subject or leaves the room. I don't know if you've noticed, but the Peet apartment doesn't have any photos of her, and they don't say her name. They just say…'her.' It was like Rueben completely shut that part of himself down afterward."

Aki rested her palm on her chin and listened. Martha hoped she heard what she was saying.

"You see, Rueben can handle a lot. But being abandoned, he can't deal with that."

Aki leaned back in her chair and sipped her drink. "That's why he stays with Marshall. Because he has abandonment issues."

Martha nodded. Her point was getting through. "Exactly. Marshall is…Marshall. Rueben stays with him because he knows what it feels like, and he can't put anyone else through that. He's like that."

Aki narrowed her eyes and thoughtfully studied the top of the glass conservatory. She looked like she wanted to say more, but Webber interrupted them. "May I refill your drinks, ladies?"

They both looked down at their drinks and saw that they were almost empty. Martha stirred the strawberry slush in the bottom of her glass. "No, Webber, I think I've had enough."

Aki pushed her glass away. "That's enough for me, too."

He grabbed the glasses with quick, jerky movements. "Excellent. Might I suggest a dip in the pool or maybe the jacuzzi? We offer an excellent selection of women's swimwear designed to fit your unique figures."

Martha snorted in laughter. Whoever had written Webber's script wasn't much of a writer. "Thanks, Webber. I think we're good."

Aki turned to Martha. "You sure? I think we're all stuck here for the night, or at least most of it, anyway. It might do us good to get in the water for a bit and relax. We've had a big day."

Martha shrugged. Aki was right. They couldn't exactly go back to their houses with all those reporters. At least not right now, anyway. They might as well enjoy their stay here at Casa del Buzz.

Martha sat with Aki in the hot tub and let the warm water massage her joints. God, it felt so good after the week they'd had.

Feeling more relaxed than she had in a while, Martha started telling old cop stories she'd heard. For only having been on the force for over a year now, she had a lot of them. The guys loved to tell them in the break room.

"Then there was the time Tom and some of the other officers went after this guy...a known drug dealer. They'd been trailing him for months. Finally, they had enough on him. He lived in this rundown apartment building. They had a warrant and everything but when they heard a scream from inside—it had been a movie on TV—they burst into his house yelling, guns drawn, and the dude was asleep. Ass-naked."

Aki winced. "Ah. That's awful."

"Yep. He was, like, old and wrinkled, too. Flabby ass."

Aki groaned and covered her face.

"So they had him at gunpoint, you know, and he's all yelling, and the cops were all yelling with guns out. And instead of, you know, asking if he can put on some clothes or something like that…the dude's a runner."

"Yikes. With his goods all flapping about…"

"Yup."

Aki squinted.

"Not even just that. This guy… Before he runs, he reaches down and grabs a random pile of clothes off the floor and splits for the patio door. The officers were all yelling at him to stop, and the man does a running start, then he jumps over the second-floor railing."

"Oh my gosh. Was he okay?"

"I guess. Once he landed, he kept running. And flapping."

"Ugh."

"Yeah. So the officers all booked it down the stairs, and by the time they got to the bottom, the guy is racing down the road on his bare feet. And it's chilly out. The officers were all wearing coats. So, he's running, and cars are honking, people are yelling. Three officers are chasing down this naked dude through alleys, and he manages to get ahead by cutting through a noodle shop's back door. All the while, according to witnesses who were eating, he's trying to put on his clothes and run at the same time."

"Yikes." Aki shook her head.

"He knew the area and had a good head start on the offi-cers, but here's the worst part. The pile of clothes he grabbed was his girlfriend's, and of course, none of it fit. Apparently, his girlfriend was young and shopped at those high school boutiques."

"Ahh…dirty old man."

"Right. So, when they finally caught him, he's this middle-aged, hairy naked dude running down the sidewalk wearing a ruffled women's top all bunched up near his armpits and pink Victoria's Secret panties halfway up his legs."

They both laughed hard, and Martha finished. "They had to cut the top off him. He couldn't get it off."

"Are you sure it was his girlfriend's clothes? Or is that just what he said?"

Martha winced and groaned, and they both laughed.

Then Buzz walked into the pool room. "Oh, hello, ladies. Great idea. Pool party!"

CHAPTER FOUR

<u>**Tuesday, May 23, 12:30 a.m.**</u>

Between the Scotch and the emotional roller coaster and the late hour, Rueben was exhausted. He met Carolyn's eyes. "Before you tell me any more, I think we should go find the others. Get them caught up too."

Carolyn nodded. "That's good thinking. I'd love to get to know them. Here, I mean. I'd love to get to know them here, in this universe."

Rueben and his friends had recently discovered a barn full of advanced tech sent out into the universes by a Buzz from another world, so Carolyn's reveal that she was from another one wasn't that big a shock. Still, Rueben couldn't believe he was only finding out about it now. And she was Pete's mom as well as his? Oh well, with an inter-dimensional emergency on their doorstep, emotional turmoil could wait.

He pulled out his phone. "This mansion is huge. There's no telling where they are." He called Martha, then Aki, but neither of them answered their phones. "I guess I'll have to give you the tour."

"I've been in several versions of this place. They're usually quite similar. Maybe I can—"

He gulped. "Well, I've been here a lot too, but I've only been to a handful of rooms. Buzz has a lot of…secrets." He knew she was only trying to help him out, but after all this time apart, her words felt overbearing. Man, living with Marshall had made him such a dick at times.

"Some things are very consistent between the universes," she mused. "You spend a lot of time with Buzz?"

"Yep, mostly here lately."

She pointed up the stairs. "Is the theater on the second floor?"

Rueben nodded.

"Maybe we could try there?"

They climbed the marble steps to the second floor, their footsteps echoing all the way. Rueben and Carolyn reached the carpeted hallway, and he briefly filled her in on his relationship with Buzz. "I found out about my time warp power a few months ago, on Valentine's Day to be exact. There was a microwave bomb that took out half the people in New York City, and I died for the first time."

Her face turned serious for a moment. Then she laughed. "The first time's always the hardest."

"You're telling me. Scared the shit out of me. Thought I was losing my mind. Buzz was the only person I could think of who might be able to explain it to me. He knows a lot about science."

She winked. "I know."

She took in the plush carpeted hallway and the bronze busts of famous scientists standing at every few feet. She stopped at a full-size rendering of Albert Einstein. "It's always a mystery to me how science makes this much money."

"When you're as smart as Buzz, it pays."

"In my universe, it was video game tech."

"Hm, same here," Rueben said.

"I figured." Carolyn stared at the Einstein statue and nodded slowly. "And knowing what I know about Buzz, I can see why you'd turn to him for help."

Rueben dug his hands into his pockets. "Yeah. The funny thing is, he believed me almost right away. We've spent a lot more time together over the last few months. We brought Martha into our little crew because we needed to stop the microwave bomb from detonating, and she had some useful information and a killer cop instinct. Also, her déjà vu helped us. I guess she's kind of like Organic Jim and Thorne but on a much lesser scale. She's not crazy."

Carolyn nodded. "Trying to understand our warping ability can certainly make a person's head spin."

Rueben chuckled. "When we were dealing with Pete, Buzz created a list of rules regarding time warping. 'Buzz's Rules for Repeaters.'" He paused when Carolyn gave him a curious look. "After you tell us your story, I have a feeling we'll have to add some more rules."

They approached the ornate oak doors leading into the theater. The doorknobs were dual bronze carvings of roaring lions.

He opened the theater. Martha and Aki weren't in there, but Carolyn was in awe of the room. Even he couldn't blame her. He couldn't help but marvel every time he stepped inside. Red velvet curtains. Plush seats. Gold carvings on the walls. Ultra-modern track lights on the ceiling.

She stared up at the massive screen. "Wow. I'd love to see something in here."

Rueben laughed. "Yeah, well, all Buzz ever watches in here

are science documentaries. And not even the interesting ones. The really bad ones that only professionals would even understand, let alone appreciate."

She laughed, and they headed back downstairs.

Rueben told her, "If they're not in the theater, it's possible they're in the pool room, decompressing. We did have a long day."

They took the stairs down, back toward the living room, and down several halls toward the indoor pool room.

"So, Aki," Carolyn said. "You two?"

Rueben shuddered. His mom had just come back into his life, and he wasn't comfortable having the "Who are you dating?" talk.

"I can tell you care about her. She cares about you too."

"How can you tell?" The words fell out of his mouth.

Carolyn gave a motherly smile. "It's obvious by the way she touches your arm. I saw when I first approached the two of you outside the U.N. building. She must have thought I was another crazy reporter at first."

"Oh." It felt good to have some confirmation that Aki was still into him. Although not nearly as bad as Buzz, Rueben wasn't the best at reading the opposite sex and at times wondered why Aki was still hanging around a computer geek like him regardless of him being a "mysterious and badass" Repeater.

"How did you meet her? Work?"

Rueben nodded. "I…uh needed her professional help with stopping the bomb. Then our work relationship kinda turned into a, um, personal relationship."

She must have sensed his reticence, because she didn't comment further on it. Instead, she changed the subject.

"What do you do for the government? Here. On this world, I mean."

"It's not the same in all the universes?"

Carolyn shook her head. "In one world, you're the head of the CIA. That timeline was a bit farther along in years though. In another, you were a field agent and your best friend was Mike—"

"Don't say it."

"Fury."

"Argh. I used to hate that guy. He's okay now though. I guess."

"Ahh, then you must be in the CIA's IT department."

"Yeah, how did you know?"

"In most worlds, you're in the IT department, and you hate Fury. In a lot of the other worlds, you two get along quite nicely. Whatever did he do to deserve your ire?"

He smirked and delivered a line he'd always wanted to. "If I tell you, I'd have to kill you."

She shrugged. "Go ahead, fine by me."

They chuckled at the inside Repeater joke. Rueben was surprised by how good it felt to be laughing with his mom, even at a time like this. When he glanced up, he saw that they'd reached the pool room entrance. From the other side came the muted sound of rock music. After a curious glance at Carolyn, he opened the door.

The pool room was a large circular room with high glassed walls and colored lights. The floor above it contained an observatory, and Buzz had all sorts of telescopes up there. Tonight, Martha, Aki, and Buzz were all in the water. Rueben had never known that Buzz had a great sound system installed in here. Right now, the volume was high and pumped out party rock as the three of them sat in the warm water, beers everywhere.

Rueben yelled over the music, "Hey, Buzz. I didn't hear you get in."

Buzz lounged against the side of the hot tub with his scrawny arms draped over the rim, reminding Rueben of Ferris Bueller. He sipped from a beer bottle, and Rueben wanted to laugh at the image of Party Buzz.

"I just got here. Came in through the back. Had to put the surviving Binnies back in their rooms."

"Where's Zach?"

Buzz winked. "He went home with a busty reporter. Him and Mike Fury both. The lucky bastards. It was my plan on the rooftop that prevented the worst of the devastation those drones could've caused. But did the reporters want to hear about me? Oh no. All they were interested in were boobs and muscle. People are stupid."

They all laughed at that and consoled Buzz's ego. Buzz seemed happy for the praise and waved Rueben and Carolyn closer to the pool. "Get in. The water's fine. We saved the world, and we should be celebrating, damn it."

They all cheered, and Buzz continued, "We can also toast to the return of Carolyn Peet." He made a face. "That is unless you plan on bailing again."

Carolyn shifted uncomfortably on her feet, and Martha and Aki stared at a clueless Buzz. Aki snapped her fingers at him. "Hey, shut up."

Carolyn laughed awkwardly. "No. It's okay. I deserved that."

Rueben held up a palm. "Guys. I know we've had a hell of a day. But Carolyn has some important stuff to say." When his friends didn't visibly react, Rueben added, "About Pete."

They all stiffened. Buzz's beer tipped out of his hand and spilled into the water like urine.

Rueben cleared his throat as Martha and Aki climbed out. "Can we kill the music?"

Buzz reluctantly shut off the music and climbed out after the girls.

Rueben tossed his buddy a beach towel sitting off to the side. "You all might need another drink. This is going to be a lot to take in."

CHAPTER FIVE

Tuesday, May 23, 1:17 a.m.

Now mostly dried off and wearing white silky guest robes that Buzz had for them, they filtered into the living room.

Rosa had been watching a soap opera, but she flipped off the TV. "Ay, Mr. Buzz, maybe tomorrow we will find out if Pedro survives."

Buzz leaned against a couch. "Again? What happened to Pedro this time? He didn't try to fake his death again, did he?"

She shook her head vigorously. "Oh, it was terrible. His new wife found him in bed with another woman, so she pushed him through the window. He smashed right through the glass and fell from the third story. Then…"

She gasped and held her hand over her heart. "Then roll credits! Ay! Now we have to know if he made it. Especially because he has a secret love child that is on her way to find him after the cartel killed her mother. Now, the father she never knew might be dead too. Dios mio!"

She clasped her palms around her cheeks and shook her

head. "Oh, Mr. Buzz. I prepared a special tart. Would you like to sample it?"

Buzz lit a cigar and cocked his head. "Sounds good. Could you bring coffee and snacks for our guests? We've all imbibed quite a bit tonight. I think food might do us all good."

When the doorbell suddenly rang, Buzz frowned. "Hm, must be those Bible thumpers again trying to change my mind on evolution. Rosa, check the door, too?"

"Of course. Bring snacks and answer the door." The maid padded off to the kitchen, and Buzz and Rueben shared a smile. Carolyn pointed toward where Rosa had gone. "You still have Rosa?"

Buzz looked at her curiously. "Still?" He turned to Rueben. "This really is going to be a lot to take in, isn't it?"

Rueben nodded.

Buzz turned to Carolyn. "All right, Carolyn, you have the floor."

Carolyn clasped her hands together and pursed her lips. For a time, the room remained silent. "I honestly don't know where to begin." She glanced at Rueben, and he nodded for her to go on. "Obviously, all of you know that Rueben has… certain powers?" They all nodded. "And you all have met, of course, future Rueben from another world. I believe you call him Pete?"

They all nodded as Rosa appeared with lemon tarts arranged on a silver platter as well as a coffee carafe. She poured everyone a cup. "Mr. Buzz, there was no one at the door. They must have left. Want me to check the security cameras?"

"Nah. Those people are harmless." Buzz dismissed her and Rosa left the room.

Carolyn sipped her coffee, and they took small bites of the

tart as she continued her story. "Pete and I… we are from a different universe." She paused as if expecting Martha, Aki, and Buzz to gasp but they only nodded. "A parallel one, to be exact. One that's a bit further along on the timeline. Twenty years in the future."

Martha was the first to speak. "We found a barn that another Buzz had somehow transported throughout the multiverse." She bit her lip. "Do we all exist in other universes?"

"Yes."

"Then Rueben…he can 'warp' in all of them?" Buzz asked.

"No," Carolyn said. "Out of all the parallel worlds, only two Ruebens can warp." She nodded at Rueben. "The Rueben from this world and the Rueben from my world. Pete, as you call him."

"Very interesting," Buzz said. "I'll add this to my Rules for Repeaters. Can anyone else warp? Besides Pete and Rueben."

Carolyn shook her head. "No. As far as I know, the Ruebens and I are the only ones."

Martha and Aki gasped. Buzz cocked an eyebrow. "You're a Repeater, too?"

"Yes. From everything I can tell, it's hereditary."

"I knew it." Buzz raised a triumphant fist. Everyone looked at him. "Ahh, sorry. Go on."

Rueben raised a hand to stop her. "If it's hereditary, then where did you get it, Mom? Did either of your parents act strangely? Like they could've been warping back in time while you were a kid?"

Carolyn shook her head. "As far as I can tell, no. They were normal. And so were my grandparents. But I don't know. Maybe they hid it well like I did with you. Or, maybe they never died early enough to find out that they would warp back in time afterward. Maybe...they just died of old age without ever knowing."

Following her cop's intuition, Martha narrowed her eyes. "How did you get here? If your universe is farther along than ours, why do you look around Marshall and Pete's age? Shouldn't you be older than Pete?"

Carolyn looked flushed. "Ahh, well, you see, I'll have to go back to the beginning." She gripped her glass and stared into the dark liquid as she spoke. "Many years ago, our Earth... died. Rueben—I mean, Pete and I warped back and tried to save it. So, so many times, we tried. Buzz, you were there. You tried to help us."

"Cool. Am I hot there?"

Aki threw a pillow at Buzz.

"Actually," Carolyn said, "you had plastic surgery back on my Earth." When Buzz's eyebrows raised curiously, Carolyn scrunched up her face. "It didn't turn out too well for you in my opinion." She glanced down at her cup and smiled. "All of you are mostly the same in every universe. Sometimes you make different choices here and there that affect your trajectory in small ways. Overall, you're mostly the same."

Martha raised her hand. "So, this other Earth is the real Earth? This one is the fake one?"

Rueben interjected. "Well, I don't think the word 'real' applies here. I think everything is real. We're just, like she said, in a different parallel version of the same Earth."

Buzz nodded sagely and puffed on his cigar.

Carolyn continued. "In 'my' world—"

Rueben interrupted her. "How about this? How about we give it a name? Like, say we call your world Earth-Z. And we'll call this one Earth-A."

Aki nodded. "I like Earth-Z. It makes sense."

Buzz frowned. "I would've used Greek terminology, but go on."

Carolyn continued. "So Earth-Z, as I guess we're calling it, suffered destruction. Rueben on that world, we'll call him Rueben-Z, and myself, we tried to Repeat and save Earth-Z time and time again. Nothing we did worked."

"What kind of destruction are we talking about?" Buzz said.

Carolyn shuddered. "It's…it's like a withering growth that spreads rapidly throughout the world, shriveling all life—plants and animals alike. I've never seen anything like it. It spreads and spreads until the entire world is a lifeless husk and Rueben-Z and I are the only two left alive."

"Hell of an epidemic," Buzz mused. "All biological life shrivels up and dies?"

Carolyn nodded. "Turns into dust."

Martha shook her head sadly. "That's awful." Aki nodded.

"But what's causing it?" Buzz said.

Rueben's eyes widened. "Every living creature withers to dust?" When Carolyn nodded, Rueben said, "Like the passage of a very long amount of time? Like a…time disease?"

"Time disease, eh?" Buzz chewed that over. "I like it, buddy. Some unknown phenomenon ages all living organisms at an exponentially accelerated rate until they simply turn to dust."

Carolyn touched her chin with a thoughtful look on her face. "Hmm. I never thought about it like that before."

Buzz continued. "It would explain why you and Rueben-Z are unaffected by the effects. You both are Repeaters and thus may be immune to its effects, unlike us paltry mortals." He flashed her and Rueben a jealous grin.

"If that is what's really going on, this...changes things," Carolyn said. "A time disease."

Buzz eyed her closely. "You mean to say my doppelgänger on your world never surmised that?"

"This 'phenomenon' as you put it does not act like any known disease. It behaves more like a storm or some part of the environment." Her shoulders sagged as she exhaled loudly. "Like a living curse."

Aki cleared her throat. "When does this time disease or whatever it is start to attack your Earth?"

Now Buzz leaned forward on his arms. "Yes. What seems to be the trigger for the disease?"

"We're not exactly sure," Carolyn said exasperatedly. "One day it just gets airborne somehow and starts killing every living thing. It starts in different places. When we warp back farther, it happens even sooner than the last time. As if it's following us." She dropped her gaze to the floor. "You could see why we thought it more like a curse than a disease."

Buzz shook his head. "And I went along with that notion? I find it hard to believe there's a version of me that believes in curses."

Carolyn sipped her coffee and shifted uneasily on her seat. "You would be correct. Buzz on my world, Buzz-Z, if you will...he tried what he could. But this time disease. It scared him. Badly. The phenomenon just wasn't predictable, except that it kept happening sooner and sooner with each warp back in time Rueben-Z and I did. He did, however, have an idea."

Buzz urged her to continue.

"He postulated that perhaps that world couldn't be saved—at least not on its timeline. What he suggested was that if we could hop to a parallel universe, maybe then we could figure out a way to undo and fix everything back home."

"How is that even possible?" Martha asked.

Buzz uttered something under his breath, and Aki, who'd been watching him, said, "Space and time capsule?"

Buzz nodded.

So did Carolyn. "Exactly. About twenty years earlier, Buzz-Z had been tinkering with a prototype capsule. Kinda looked like Superman's Kryptonian rocket only with more than one seat. He started working on it again when the phenomenon struck, and he devised a 'theoretical' way to jump from our Earth to other parallel Earths."

"That's incredible," Aki said.

Buzz made a hurry-up gesture. "You jumped worlds then?"

"We did. Rueben-Z and I. It was…well, you can imagine how disorienting arriving on a parallel world might be." Carolyn watched as everyone nodded and exchanged glances. "Long story short, Rueben-Z and I couldn't find anything that could help on any of the worlds we visited. No matter what we did, no matter how many Buzzes we consulted with, we were unable to save Earth-Z when we returned. Even worse, each parallel world we visited inevitably suffered the same… time disease. As if the phenomenon was following us."

"Like a curse," Martha whispered.

Carolyn drew a breath and wiped her hand across her forehead.

Buzz gestured with his cigar. "Surely you had a working idea of what was causing it."

"We thought the 'curse' was one of two things: an extremely powerful and deadly virus that could kill all life on Earth or some kind of alien invasion. We couldn't prove either so we weren't sure which it could be."

Rueben eyed his mom. "An alien invasion?"

Carolyn shrugged helplessly. "It's just that it's unlike anything we know, so we thought it must be alien. At the same time, Buzz-Z used every known instrument possible to detect the presence of aliens—and found nothing. Which scared him even more."

Buzz tapped his fingertips together. "Artificial virus, perhaps? Pathogen evolution gone wrong? Maybe advanced technology from twenty years in the future..." Buzz ordered his thoughts internally for a moment and asked, "What exactly did I—and by 'I,' I mean Buzz-Z—do to try and stop the phenomenon?"

"Do you want a list?"

"I do," Buzz said soberly.

"Okay, I'll try to think back and write you out a list. For now, know that the only true breakthrough he had was figuring out the space and time capsule to jump universes."

His face lit up. "So Buzz-Z went with you and Rueben-Z to this Earth?"

"Actually, no. You didn't want to go. You stayed on Earth-Z and perished with everyone else, waiting for us to return, earlier and earlier in the timeline with a possible solution."

"Shit," Aki said. "That must have been hard to leave him."

Carolyn wiped a tear from her eyes.

"Mom." Rueben bit his lip. "I think you're burying the lead here. What," he hesitated, "what happened to Rueben-Z? I mean, he's driven by fury and near-insanity. Why is he...well, why is he like how he is now?"

Carolyn took a calming breath. "We jumped to countless parallel Earths in our search for the solution. At first, we didn't understand that we were carrying the phenomenon with us to each one. Later we did. We realized we'd been inadvertently causing the deaths of billions.

"Rueben-Z…now, understand that it was hard for us both. We thought that we could find a way to reverse all the damage on all Earths we'd been to. We just had to find the solution. It was my fault, but I should have paid more attention to Rueben-Z. He…hid his anguish well. Eventually, one day he just…I don't know. Suffered a complete mental breakdown."

Everyone winced.

Rueben was glad that things were starting to make sense now.

Carolyn continued. "I stayed with Rueben-Z. He was my son. But his anxiety and furor seemed to grow every time he died and warped back in time. He grew almost…psychotic. The only thing that seemed to reset his symptoms was when we hopped to a new Earth. It was as if being on a new world reset both the time disease and his insanity. After jumping, he'd be more rational. I could reason with him. Talk to him."

Wow, Rueben thought. This had to be so hard on his mom to say all this. How long had she been holding it all in? Anyone she tried to talk to about it on all those Earths was doomed to die at the hand of the time disease.

"On one Earth," Carolyn said, "Buzz pinpointed that Rueben-Z was transmitting the time disease to each of the worlds. Don't ask me how he determined it, but he said that Rueben-Z was the cause, and not me even though we were both going to the same worlds." Carolyn shuddered.

"Rueben-Z was so furious that he strangled Buzz to death right in front of me." Everyone gasped. "He immediately warped back to before that, but I knew right then and there that Rueben-Z was beyond my help. The universes were beyond my help.

"You can say that I…gave up on my mission. Accepted defeat. I was so weary. All those deaths I'd seen. Since I knew I wasn't the cause, I hatched an idea that I still haven't forgiven myself for."

"You decided to leave Rueben-Z," Aki said.

"Yes." Carolyn was fighting back tears now. "We had only one space and time capsule. By that point, I was familiar with all the controls—I knew how to pilot it to other Earths. So I waited until Rueben-Z was asleep. Then I snuck onto the capsule and left that world in the dead of night." She drew a shallow breath and wiped the sweat from her forehead.

"Earth-A wasn't the first Earth I stopped at once I left Rueben-Z behind. But once I found Earth-A and decided it's where I wanted to stay, I…self-destructed the space and time capsule in case there was any way that Rueben-Z could locate it."

Rueben massaged both his temples with his thumbs. "Wow, mom, I didn't know. I didn't know any of that. It's amazing you're holding together at all after what you've been through."

"Yes," Buzz agreed, studying Carolyn. "But you never addressed the original question. Rueben-Z appears to be in his mid-forties. And…" He gestured at her body. "You also look mid-forty-ish." He ignored Martha's and Aki's indignant glances at him outing a woman's age. "Care to explain?"

Carolyn sighed. "I can try. Although it's really just a guess. The Carolyn on this Earth—Earth-A—died when she was young." Rueben started, as did Martha. "She didn't have the Repeater gene, which is consistent with the Carolyns on the other parallel worlds I've been to. And somehow—I don't know how—when I arrived on this Earth, I…grew younger. I reverted to the age she would have been if she never died. It's like I…took her place."

Buzz nodded matter-of-factly. "Temporal displacement."

Rueben, Martha, and Aki gave Buzz confused looks.

"It goes like this: the multiverse is populated by infinite copies of us, all living our lives fairly uniformly. Like Carolyn said, we might make different decisions to change things slightly, but for the most part, parallel universes are exactly that: parallel." He gestured with the butt of his cigar. "So if one were to jump from Universe A to Universe B, two of you now exist in the same world."

Rueben eyed Buzz. "And if we touch, one explodes, or there's a rip in the reality of space."

Buzz shook his head. "You've been watching *The One* with Jet Li again. No…it's more of a *Rick and Morty* situation. The two of you can interact, talk, hang out. But if one of the universes doesn't have you there, you take that person's place on their timeline until you jump again."

"*Quantum Leap?*" Rueben offered.

"Exactly, except you can only occupy yourself. Temporal displacement. That's what Carolyn did. Carolyn-A no longer existed on Earth-A so Carolyn-Z 'replaced' herself on this Earth. And will continue to do so until she leaves. Fascinating. What happened next?"

Carolyn continued. "Seeing I had a second chance at life—and was twenty years younger—I did the only thing I could think of doing. I tried to enjoy life. I made some friends. Then I let slip about my powers, and I spent some time in a psych ward.

"After that mess, I went looking for the love of my life. Marshall." She smiled at the memory. "He was the sweetest guy. He always is, in every universe. A bit dorky, awkward, and utterly loveable."

"Marshall?" Aki said.

"Yes."

Martha tilted her head in confusion. "*Marshall*, Mar*shall*?"

"Yes. He was at New York State, studying computer engineering. I soon got a job at the college coffee shop, planning to take it slow and meet Marshall. The way he asked me out was the sweetest thing. He was so shy and awkward, and he spilled his coffee all over me."

Buzz snorted. "That was a play, you know."

Carolyn blushed. "Oh, please. Marshall? In those days, that poor guy wouldn't know game if it walked up and introduced itself."

They all laughed, and Rueben scratched his head trying to imagine Marshall all love-struck and awkward. He would have to agree with Buzz on that—it was probably a play.

Carolyn's face took on a dreamy look. "He took me swing dancing because that was a thing back then. He was a pretty good dancer. Afterward, he was a total gentleman and dropped me off at my door with a sweet little kiss."

Rueben cleared his throat. "You're talking about Marshall Peet, right? From Earth-A?"

She laughed. "I know, he changed a lot when he graduated from the police academy, but that sweet little softie was still there. I think I might have been the only one in the world who saw it. So, eventually, we got married, and Rueben-A was born—"

"Whoa, whoa, whoa." Rueben waved both hands in front of him agitatedly. "You had already given birth to Rueben-Z on Earth-Z, and you happened to have an identical baby twenty years earlier on Earth-A? I'm no scientist, but I mean, the chances of that happening…out of all the different sperm and egg combinations—"

"Temporal displacement," Buzz said. "It seems you were fated to be born in this world as in all the other worlds, to keep them parallel."

Rueben scratched behind his head. "Yeah. But…"

"At least that's my best guess at the moment. I am an observer of facts. Carolyn came here. Your parents did it. You were born." Buzz turned to Carolyn to resume.

"After Rueben-A was born, I finally started to forget about the horrors of Earth-Z and abandoning Rueben-Z, as crazy as that seems. And it seemed that for once in a long time, I was going to get to live a normal life again and raise a happy little family. That was the way it was until…until Thorne came into our lives. Like I explained to Rueben, I died over five hundred times trying to save him from Thorne."

Martha rubbed at her cheek. "Wait, you knew Thorne?"

Carolyn smiled. "He wanted my Repeat power. He hijacked the bus to get to me because he thought I could give it to him. He called me 'Hopper' because he had déjà vu-like abilities. He could see events in the timeline that happened before I warped back."

Martha turned a shade paler. "Thorne was like me?"

"On a much more magnified scale," Carolyn said. "I don't think you have anything to worry about. On Earth-A, you're not crazy."

After a sigh, the color started to return to Martha's face.

"Thorne was why I felt that I had to leave Rueben and Marshall, to keep them safe from me and my power. I know now that it wasn't the right decision. At the time I kept thinking that what if Thorne's ravings had gotten noticed by the government or fringe scientists? If someone like that would've gotten their hands on me…well, who knows. They could've locked me up in a padded room for the rest of my natural life as they slowly vivisected me to try to find out how to duplicate my power."

"Sheesh," Buzz said. "That's heavy."

Carolyn sighed. "So I dropped everything in my life and ran away. I figured everything would be fine and balance itself out." She shook her head slowly, her eyes weary.

"But Rueben-Z found you," Rueben said.

"Yes. He found a way to leave the world I had abandoned him on and tracked me down. Now everything is out of balance. I should have known I couldn't outrun my past."

They were all quiet for several minutes, then Aki's face went taut. "The phenomenon that destroyed Earth-Z. The time disease. It's coming for us, now, here on Earth-A, isn't it?"

Carolyn dropped her head into her hands. "Since Rueben-Z is the carrier of it, I can only assume so. I am so, so sorry."

Martha clenched her fist. "What is Rueben-Z's game here? Why did he want to cause a global nuclear war?"

Rueben rubbed his jaw. "If he thought that the phenomenon was some type of super pathogen…"

"He might have thought he could destroy enough of the living organisms on this world before the phenomenon could take root," Buzz finished.

Aki shrugged. "It's an idea. Not a great one. But it is one."

"Well," Rueben said, "I worked it out in my head that the only reason I would do what he was trying to do was if I had to make the least worst decision from a handful of bad decisions. I guess World War III was it."

Martha drummed her fingers on her lap. "That's definitely bad."

"Hmm," Buzz said. "In the case of a global nuclear war, I'd estimate that enough people would survive the fallout in spread-out clusters throughout the planet. It would devastate the global ecosystem, but in time, we could rebuild. Kind of genius really, from an evil genius's perspective…" Upon receiving a stern look from Martha, he added, "But the very idea of it is simply too diabolical to try. Even as a Plan Z, as you will."

Carolyn picked up where Buzz had left off. "If it turns out the phenomenon is due to an alien invasion, global nuclear war would probably make our planet utterly undesirable. They'd leave us alone."

The word "alone" echoed in Rueben's mind. He was getting a better picture of Rueben-Z's mental state. The man was still out there and was an immensely bigger threat than any of them could have previously guessed now that they knew about the time disease he'd inadvertently carried to this world.

Suddenly someone called, "Hey, I have a question."

They all whipped around to see Marshall standing at the back of the room.

"Once we deal with this 'Rueben-Z mess,'" Marshall continued, "are you planning on bailing again?"

CHAPTER SIX

<u>**Tuesday, May 23, 2:33 a.m.**</u>

Marshall stood at the back of the living room with his hands in his jean pockets, his eyes looking right through Carolyn.

"H-hello, Marshall."

"Carolyn."

"How, how much of that did you hear?"

Rueben could see the anguish on his mother's face. Her face said that she wanted to run up to Marshall and embrace him, and Marshall's face... Well, it told her that she better not try.

"Enough," Marshall muttered. He scratched his jaw.

"How'd you get in here?" Buzz asked.

"I snuck inside after the maid answered the door."

Carolyn looked heartbroken. "I'm so sorry, Marshall. I didn't mean to. I should have told you—"

"Save it," Marshall said disinterestedly.

Rueben winced at the sudden tension in the room. His friends, he noticed, were in similar positions of discomfort.

Marshall was a dick, but in his defense, he had just heard that his wife was from another world where she was also married to him. Who only knew what was going through that thick skull of his.

"Oh, what's this? Some kinda fancy pie?" Marshall moved toward the remnants of tart on the silver platter. He raised a slice to his mouth and made a face. "Hm, bitter."

Rosa appeared from the doorway Marshall had just entered with a concerned look on her face, but Buzz waved her off.

Carolyn rubbed her forehead. "Marshall, can we not do this now?"

"What are we doing? I'm standing here with a bunch of Rueben's friends in a mansion you can't find with GPS—luckily I've been here before. Just standing here talking. Oh, and my wife I haven't seen in fifteen years is here too. Talking about world-hopping when all along I just thought she could warp back in time…"

"It's not like that."

"Oh? What's it like? I know you had your reasons, but feel like taking a trip down memory lane with me? Finding out what you missed during your little time away?"

Rueben groaned. His mom had just gotten done explaining how sweet Marshall had been and for a moment, he'd thought that maybe Marshall's attitude would turn a one-eighty when he next saw Carolyn. But no. Still rude-ass surly Marshall. The last thing Rueben wanted at this moment was Marshall unveiling embarrassing childhood secrets in front of his friends…particularly Aki. "Damnit, Dad. Can you not do this here?"

Marshall ignored him. "The kid had dentist appointments, homework, soccer practice."

Rueben muttered, "I never played soccer."

Marshall kept going. "Grocery shopping, laundry."

Rueben cleared his throat. "I did all of that."

Marshall still didn't acknowledge him. "On top of me having to climb the career ladder so I could keep putting food on the table and a roof over our heads. I sure could have used some help, Carolyn. Would have made things a hell of a lot easier."

"I know, Marshall, and I'm sorry. I made the best decision I could with—"

He interrupted her. "We could have handled your 'situation' together. If you'd only told me the full story…" He shook his head. "I thought marriage meant life partners. I guess that whole ''til death do us part' thing is a bit tricky for you time-hopping Repeaters."

Carolyn stared into the carpet. "Marshall, I'm sorry it's been so hard on you. I thought I explained everything I needed to at the time, and I thought we agreed that it was best."

Rueben's mouth dropped. They had agreed?

"Agreed? We talked about the possibility of you leaving for a little while until things calmed down. Then you took off and left me a goddamned letter about parallel universes and regrets. It made no sense to me, and you never gave me half a chance to ask questions."

Her eyes brimmed with tears while Marshall maintained a scowl.

"And after what I did to Thorne…God."

"You didn't have to," Carolyn said. "We could have kept—"

"I did it for you. I did it for us. I trusted you. I trusted you." Marshall's eyes twitched at the corners, and his jaw tightened.

Rueben jumped up. This was enough. "Dad, calm down. There's more to this than you think."

Marshall finally turned to him, his eyes hot and fiery. "You shut the hell up for once. I am not interested in what you have to say about my marriage."

"Your marriage? It's just as much about my childhood as it is your marriage."

"Damn it. You stay in your goddamned lane. This is between my wife and me."

Rueben turned to Aki. "I'm leaving."

Aki rose from the couch. "Maybe we should all leave."

Martha grabbed her purse from beside her.

Carolyn whimpered. "Marshall. I told you something else in that letter. It will always be just you and me."

Marshall's voice cracked. "Yeah, but it wasn't."

Rueben's eyes widened at the abrupt softening of his dad. He stopped. They all stopped and watched. All of a sudden, Marshall began to sob. "It wasn't you and me. It was just me. All alone. And I... I..." Marshall collapsed on the couch, and he wept.

Rueben's face paled. He had never seen his dad cry. The closest he'd ever seen was him misting up during the national anthem at a football championship. But this... Rueben didn't know what this was.

Carolyn rushed over to her husband and wrapped her arms around him, and he sobbed, "I missed you so much. I just missed you." Marshall grabbed her neck and pulled her closer to him. Then they sat, and he kissed her wet cheeks and leaned his forehead against hers.

She cried with him. "I missed you, too."

Rueben stared at his parents weeping on his best friend's couch.

Whoa. And he thought time-jumping blew his mind.

Martha turned to him. "I'm pretty sure it's the end of the world now. Marshall's crying. We're fucked."

Rueben and his friends laughed softly, uneasily.

At that moment, a shrieking alarm filled the house. Everyone clapped their hands over their ears.

Buzz's body went rigid. "The security alarm. It's a break-in."

CHAPTER SEVEN

<u>Tuesday, May 23, 3:12 a.m.</u>

Snapping to attention, Buzz rushed over to a side table and snatched up a tablet. A few swipes later, he'd pulled up some security video feeds from around the mansion. While Marshall helped Carolyn up from the couch, Rueben's friends gathered around Buzz to peer at the footage. Martha and Aki, still in their bathrobes, grabbed their handguns from their piles of dry clothes.

Then the screaming alarms died as suddenly as they'd begun.

Buzz frowned. "What the hell?"

Rueben waved his hand in front of Buzz's face to get his attention. "Has it ever malfunctioned like that?"

"No. I designed it myself. My designs never malfunction. Oh shit."

"What?" Rueben said. "Did it malfunction?" That's when he saw the figure on the security feed making its way through the halls of Buzz's mansion. "Oh shit."

"Pete, er, Rueben-Z," Aki said.

"Shit," Martha agreed. "How did he find this place?"

Footsteps sounded outside the open doorway, and a moment later, Rueben-Z stepped inside the living room with a ferocious grin on his face. He no longer wore his white hoodie with stripes on the shoulders. Now he wore jeans and a black compression shirt underneath his form-fitting metallic body armor.

Tiny lights blinked on parts of the armor and he had some kind of streamlined metal tube running alongside each arm, connected to it. The scar on one half of his face gleamed in the room's lighting.

"Hello, *friends*. I should've known you'd all be lying low here. Nice digs. Just like on all the other Earths. But you should know, there's no safety in numbers. There's only death."

He laughed harshly, and Rueben stepped forward between his friends and Rueben-Z. "Death for you. Or have you forgotten that you can't warp anymore? If you die, you don't get to come back."

Rueben-Z sneered. "Oh, I haven't forgotten. Thanks for that. You fucking bastard. But being able to die does put things into perspective. Really gets you to focus on what's important. You know. Like revenge."

Carolyn stifled a sob from somewhere behind Rueben, but he kept his attention on Rueben-Z. "You don't have to exact revenge or hurt or kill anyone. We know what you've been through and we can help you—"

"Oh? You know, do you?" Rueben-Z's eyes landed on Carolyn. "Mother? So good of you to join us. My, aren't you looking young and spry again? What are you? Younger than me now? Same age? Oh, how the surprises keep coming. And father? You're here too? And been sobbing like a baby?" He scoffed. "Pathetic."

Marshall steeled himself and stepped in front of Carolyn. "You're no son of mine. You need to leave. Now."

"Oh? Do I?"

Marshall glanced at Rueben and his friends, then back at Rueben-Z. "Be smart about this. We outnumber you."

Fear crept over Rueben-Z's face. But it was only a feint. Without looking, he pressed a button on his futuristic body armor, and a moment later, two burly men in red plaid shirts and beards who looked like they could have been lumberjacks barreled into the room and stopped at either side of Rueben-Z. All they were missing were axes, but judging by their meaty fists, they wouldn't need weapons.

Upon seeing them, Buzz slapped his head. "Oh no."

"Oh yes," Rueben-Z said. "I broke into one of your hidden storage garages. Thanks for the robotic partners, *buddy*. And also the new gear." He angled his head at the metal tubes fixed under his arms.

Rueben set his jaw. "Uh, Buzz. Robotic partners. Gear. What's he talking about?"

Before Buzz could respond, Rueben-Z raised one arm, and a jet of white-hot flame shot from the metal tube and spewed forth into the living room. "Enough talking. More fighting."

"Get Mom out of here," Rueben yelled at Marshall as Rueben-Z passed his flames over the living room. The heat was sweltering.

"I never abandon a fight, son. Besides, you never split the party."

"We need to get out of here, not fight." Rueben barely had time to raise a small side table in defense against Rueben-Z's flamethrower. When it grew hot, he threw it aside and dove for the cover of a brass statue of some famous scientist.

Rueben-Z harshly chuckled as he turned and started spewing flames at the doorway leading out of the room, effectively trapping them in the living room.

Marshall picked up a lamp, ripped its cord from the wall, and hurled it at Rueben-Z, who batted it aside with his forearm. "Sometimes, you have to fight. To kill."

"Please don't kill Rueben-Z," Carolyn called. "He could be the key to the cure."

Marshall grimaced and, relenting to his wife, turned to Rueben. "Well, can't you just die and repeat back to before that madman got here so we can prepare better?"

Rueben didn't want them all to have to go through Carolyn's speech again. Besides, Marshall and his mother seemed to have worked out their differences, and nobody wanted to relive that. Buzz could switch back on an automated email to let everyone know what had happened after he warped back if he chose to do so, but that might confuse his friends even more. No. He couldn't lean on his power like a crutch every time something didn't go his way.

As if Buzz was reading Rueben's mind, he called from his crouching position behind a sofa off to the side. "Don't Repeat unless you have to. From what Carolyn said, warping could play a part in the whole 'phenomenon' trigger." Buzz winced as a plume of fire shot over his head. "We don't need any more variables right now."

Great, Rueben thought. If he wasn't supposed to use his power, essentially he was as hobbled as Rueben-Z. Guess they could add a new rule to Buzz's Rules for Repeaters: *Do not warp in the presence of a Repeater infected with a time disease because it could destroy the entire world—*

A gunshot went off, and Rueben, still taking cover behind the brass statue, glanced across the room. Martha had fired a warning shot at one of the two lumberjack henchmen. "Stay back, or I'll shoot."

The burly minion either didn't hear her or didn't care. As he advanced, Rueben's stomach tightened when he saw that the second henchman was walking fearlessly toward Aki, who had her handgun out as well.

Rueben wanted to do something, but Rueben-Z had pinned him down again. The brass statue in front of him had started to melt as a horizontal column of flame poured his way.

Another gunshot went off. This time it was Aki's weapon. A *pinging* sound followed it and Aki said, "Oh shit!"

Rueben stole a glance at Aki as she fired twice more. Her bullets deflected harmlessly off the henchman advancing upon her.

"I think these guys are metal," she called as she left her hiding place and dove behind the sofa Marshall and Carolyn were crouched behind.

"Because they are," Rueben-Z roared. "A couple of Buzz's bots. I reprogrammed them."

Earlier, Rueben-Z had mentioned "robotic partners." Rueben called to Buzz, "They don't look like your kind of robots."

The lumberjack henchman who had been plodding after Aki now turned and started trudging toward Martha's position a few yards behind the other one. They moved like bulldozers. Martha fired a couple of shots that did nothing, and Aki rose from her position behind the sofa and shot one of the minions in the back of the head. The bullet deflected with a *ping*.

"Yes, they're mine," Buzz cried. "Binnie wasn't my first humanoid robot. Not all my bots have boobs, you know."

Rueben grimaced as he ducked back from another sweltering whoosh of fire. "I'm pretty sure they do, actually."

"Webber doesn't," Aki helpfully said as she crouched next to Marshall and Carolyn.

"Thank you," Buzz said.

Rueben groaned. "Can we please not discuss robot boobs as we're all about to be melted alive?"

"Son." Marshall met Rueben's eyes. "Don't let this get to your head, but I think you're right about us needing to get out of here."

"Can you repeat that, please?" Rueben knew it was immature, but damn it felt good to say that.

His dad ignored the quip and glanced at the fiery doorway. "Can't get through the exit without roasting like a Christmas goose. And it seems he knows the layout of this place. Even if we could get through the doorway, he'd probably still be able to take out at least one of us."

"Egads." Buzz wiped a hand across his sweating forehead. "We wouldn't have to escape the house. We only need to make it to the safe room. We'd need a diversion to escape this room though."

"Come out, come out, wherever you are, little piggies!" Rueben-Z shouted above the blaze of his arm flamethrower. "I'm getting bored, and this house is getting hot."

From across the room, Martha grunted as she kicked a side table into the two approaching lumberjack robots. It barely hindered them as they stomped toward her position. They were strong, but they were slow. Also, they didn't talk.

Suddenly the sofa was engulfed in flames, and Marshall and Carolyn fled to behind a loveseat near Rueben's position. Meanwhile, Aki hunkered down behind Rueben, placing a hand on his shoulder. "Your dad's right. We have to go."

"Diversion!" Buzz said to Rueben. "Now."

"I'm not a trained monkey," Rueben said.

"Sometimes, buddy, I wish you were."

With her hand still on Rueben's shoulder, Aki rose and fired another round at the minions who were almost to Martha.

"A diversion would be nice," Martha called out. "Any time now."

Diversion, Rueben thought, but all he could see was fire. *Fire. Diversion.* That's when he glanced up at the ceiling and caught the reflection of a sprinkler head. Then he saw another and another. They were all over the ceiling, cleverly hidden among the artwork there. "Buzz, why aren't the sprinklers working?"

"Fuck. I don't know. They should be."

Rueben-Z started to make his way toward Rueben's position, the heat of the flames cooking the sweat on Rueben's arms. "Ha. The intruder alarm wasn't the only thing I disabled."

Rueben had an idea. He swiveled his head and found himself face-to-face with Aki behind him. She looked so sexy with that determined look in her dark eyes and her pistol in her hand. *Her pistol...*

"Can you shoot the sprinkler system?"

She blinked. "Would that work?"

"It's worth a shot."

From across the room, Martha's gun clicked empty. "I'm all out!"

As Aki raised her gun to shoot at the ceiling, Rueben-Z turned up the intensity on the flames, and she cried out. Dropping the gun, she fell against Rueben and then rolled away from him onto the floor. The sleeve of her robe was on fire, and she worked frantically to get the garment off.

Rueben-Z's footsteps were growing closer. Aki managed to get out of the robe, but she was nowhere near her gun.

"The gun!" Marshall was shouting at Rueben. "Toss me the gun!"

Rueben reached out and scooped up the gun, but he didn't toss it to his dad. He'd put in quite the combat training when they'd prepared for the Pout mission. He raised the gun and lined up his shot on the nearest sprinkler head set into the ceiling.

"Son, what the hell are you doing?"

Rueben pulled back to the shrinking cover of the melting statue as the flames flared and intensified again.

Aki crouched back behind him, wincing from the pain of her burned arm. "By my count, there's only one bullet left. Make your shot count."

Marshall slapped his palm to his head. "We're fucked."

"Hey, you scarred up evil bastard!" It was Martha coming toward them from across the room. She raised her arm and launched her empty gun at Rueben-Z. He grunted as it struck his shoulder and he turned and spewed some fire her way.

Taking a breath, Rueben leaned out from behind the brass statue and aimed at the sprinkler head. He fired, there was a *ping*, then…nothing.

"It was worth a try, buddy," Buzz said. Then the ceiling started to rain. "All right!"

"That was a goddamn good shot," Marshall muttered as water dripped from his head. "A goddamn good shot."

Rueben-Z roared in rage.

Water continued to spray from the sprinkler system. Rueben-Z readjusted his stance and slipped in the pooling water. He roared even louder.

"To the safe room," Buzz said. "Follow me! Everything will be all right."

CHAPTER EIGHT

<u>**Tuesday, May 23, 3:31 a.m.**</u>

"Shit, shit, shit, this is bad," Buzz kept saying as he stared at his computer screen.

They were all standing in his secret server room, the very one that contained the consolidated timeline calendar of all Rueben's warps. Those synced here automatically via the nanobot Buzz had injected into Rueben. The door leading into here was reinforced and could take quite a beating if Rueben-Z decided to try to breach it, so they had some time to recover.

Rueben glanced up from Aki's arm. It was only a minor burn, but judging from her winces, it hurt pretty bad. After making sure that she was okay, Rueben stepped over to his best friend.

"What's wrong?"

"What's wrong? What's wrong? He's locked me out of all my systems."

"Pete, er—I mean Rueben-Z?" It felt weird calling his doppelgänger from another world the same name as his.

"No, the man in the fuckin' moon. Yes, of course, Rueben-Z. How's he in my system? How's he know my passwords?"

Rueben hadn't seen Buzz under this much stress in quite a while.

"He's cut the Wi-Fi and my fiber optic line and..." Buzz pulled out his smartphone. "He's blocking cell signal too? We can't even call for help—"

Rueben grabbed Buzz by both shoulders. "Hold it together, man. We're going to make it out of here, okay. Just breathe."

Buzz met his eyes for the briefest of moments and started breathing again. Just then, Rosa stepped into the room through a hidden servant's passageway with a platter containing aspirin, a beer, and a bottle of aloe. She handed the aloe to Aki and presented the aspirin and beer to Buzz.

He wasted no time in downing the pill with a swig of beer. "Rosa, I love you. Ah, much better."

"Jesus," Marshall muttered from off to the side where he stood with Carolyn and Martha. "And that guy owns a mansion?"

Aki joined Rueben and Buzz while she gingerly rubbed aloe on her arm. "Maybe we can talk to Pete—I mean, Rueben-Z. See what he wants?"

Rueben nodded. "Negotiate?"

"Exactly. I have training in dealing with terrorists."

"I think it's clear what he wants," Buzz said. "He wants to kill us. He's pissed that we took away his warping powers."

Rueben thought it over. "Yeah, but before the summit, he was only trying to get us out of the picture. He didn't want any of us to die because he knew versions of us all that died on his home world. Who only knows how many other versions of ourselves he met on the other worlds he went to and accidentally destroyed when he brought the phenomenon with him—"

Suddenly a loud *crackle* filled the room from an overhead intercom. Buzz glanced up from his computer screen.

Rueben-Z's voice came over the intercom. "I did *not* destroy all those worlds."

Rueben looked confusedly at Carolyn. Carolyn nodded. She'd answer.

"I'm sorry, but a Buzz confirmed that it was true. He said that the phenomenon was linked to you and not me."

Silence filled the room for a few moments.

"You mean the Buzz you stranded me with when you stole the space and time capsule?"

Carolyn didn't know what to say. She glanced helplessly at Rueben.

"Look," Rueben said. "Why don't we talk like normal people here?"

"Normal people?" Rueben-Z scoffed. "We're far from normal. We're gods. Well, I used to be. Maybe it's for the better…"

"Is that what you want? To die and be at peace?"

Silence. Then, "No. But I can still save this world. Just not with you and your friends opposing me."

"You'd murder them in cold blood?" Rueben said. "They're your friends."

"Hah. That's rich. I don't even know you people. You've already died on other worlds. What's different about this one?"

Aki stared down the intercom in the ceiling. "What's different is that in this one, we're going to kick your ass. You're mortal, remember?"

"Ah, Aki. So full of spunk and fight."

"We don't have to fight anymore," Carolyn blurted.

Rueben-Z sneered. "Says the mother who abandoned her son on one world, only to travel to a parallel world and abandon that son too."

Carolyn started to shake, and Marshall caught her. "Shut up, you sonofabitch, you hear me? You hear me?"

"No, you shut up, Pops. We're about the same age in this world, don't forget. I'm bigger than you now. I'm not scrawny and weak."

"I'm not afraid of you," Marshall said, but he glanced at his out-of-shape body and sighed inwardly.

Aki leaned toward Rueben and Buzz and whispered, "This guy is not just going to let us go, and I'm not sure we're going to be able to talk him down. He and his two robot minions could be right outside the room, waiting for us to try to escape."

Buzz cocked an eye at her. "Are you trying to use subtext?"

"Huh? What I'm saying is, we may need to be prepared to use deadly force."

Rueben felt like he was going to be sick to his stomach. "I don't want to kill myself. Not if we don't have to."

"Son, he's got a goddamn flamethrower, and he means business." Marshall sighed. "Your woman's got a good point. This is survival of the fittest. Is it going to be him or us?"

Off to the side, Carolyn was rubbing her eyes. Rueben clapped a hand to his head. Was it just him or was the room spinning?

Suddenly, a heavy *thud* sounded against the reinforced door to the server room. Then another. Everyone looked at each other. *Thud, thud. Thud, thud.* There were two sets of fists raining blows upon the other side.

"Those two asshole robots," Martha said. "Aki, you got any more ammo left?"

Aki shook her head. Rueben had returned her gun to her after they'd reached the safe room.

Martha turned to Buzz. "You got any ammo down here?"

"Nada. It's all up at the shooting range."

Marshall looked perplexed. "You have a shooting range? Maybe I judged you too soon."

"No." It was Rueben. "Guns don't work on the robots."

"They'd work on Rueben-Z," Martha said.

"We don't have to kill—"

"Son, the world ain't all sunshine and roses. We're not all walking out of here alive unless you warp back or kill him. A peace treaty isn't on his agenda."

Thud, thud. Thud, thud.

The blows seemed to be louder now as if the door's seal was starting to give. They didn't have much time left. Maybe their best bet was for him to die and warp back to before Rueben-Z got here, but that was a variable they didn't need, not when the time disease phenomenon seemed to be affected in some way by warping. If Rueben warped in the presence of Rueben-Z, that could jump-start the end of the world.

Rueben spotted Rosa hanging back against the wall, and he had an idea. "Rosa, you came in through a secret passage, right?"

"That is correct, Mr. Rueben."

"Did you see where that man is in the mansion?"

"I am sorry, I did not."

Thud, thud. Thud, thud.

Rosa's eyes widened, and she looked up at her master. "Mr. Buzz. I have an idea. A plan. Although you may not like it."

Buzz looked irritated. He'd already finished his beer and

had realized that he didn't have another one. "What kind of plan?"

"One inspired by my favorite soap opera."

Rueben, for one, liked Rosa's plan. Codenamed *Operation Pedro*, it involved faking their death, not so that they could run off with another lover but so that Rueben-Z would finally leave them alone. Which meant that no one had to die.

Rueben didn't want anyone to have to die. He just hoped that Marshall could fit through Rosa's secret servant's passage.

It was a tight squeeze. They'd all barely managed to wriggle inside the narrow passageway and replace the secret wall panel behind them as the reinforced door to Buzz's server room caved in with a loud *boom*.

At first, Rueben feared that the two robots might hear them moving in the passageway, but it turned out that he didn't have to worry about that. As soon as the lumberjack minions had entered the server room, they started destroying the place. At least that's what it sounded like. Computer screens *crashed* against the wall. Glass *crackled* underfoot. Wires short-circuited. Desks being overturned and slammed against the floor.

Directly in front of Rueben in the narrow passage, Rosa led the way, a flashlight held in one hand so that she could make sure they took the correct path whenever it diverged to other parts of the mansion. The rest of them held their smartphones to provide some light. Otherwise, it would have been pitch black.

Once, Aki thought she felt a spider crawling on her arm.

She bumped into Rueben and whispered for Rosa to hurry up. Finally, they came to a wall, and Rosa turned back to face them with a finger raised to her lips. In her black and white maid's outfit, the scene seemed almost comical.

They all turned off their smartphone lights, and Rosa opened the secret panel. They followed her out into a kitchen. It was mostly empty, but a few pots and pans were lying on the countertops, as well as a knife block and a marble rolling pin. The sprinklers weren't on in this part of the building so they didn't have to worry about slipping in any water.

Even though the server room was a good distance away, the sound of the rampaging robots echoed through the passageway. Rueben leaned over to Buzz and said, "I'm sorry about all your computers. I know that room meant a lot to you."

Buzz nodded grimly. "It's all saved to the cloud, but ..yeah, it was a good fortress of solitude for me. I'll miss it a lot."

"At least those two robots are occupied."

Buzz smirked. "Yep. They won't give us any more trouble. They're strong but dumb as shit."

"What's their name?"

"Bob."

Once everyone had stepped into the kitchen, Rosa stepped back into the passageway. "I shall go and release the animals. The goat and the monkey. Be safe."

Buzz nodded and motioned for everyone to follow him. They were rounding a wheeled stainless steel prep table and heading toward the doorway out when a figure stepped into the room. It was much too petite to be Rueben-Z.

"Binnie?" Buzz said. "What are you doing here?"

The sexbot wearing nothing but lingerie posed seductively in the doorway with one hand resting on the frame.

After all this time, Rueben still found it hard to believe that Buzz's Binnies were robots. Binnie stepped into the kitchen and sauntered toward them with those long, toned legs, silky smooth brown hair, and huge brown eyes with thick, voluminous lashes. Rueben couldn't take his eyes off her. There was absolutely nothing about her that indicated she was a machine.

When she passed him, she winked at him and grazed her fingertips over his leg. His heartbeat quickened. Aki gave both him and Binnie the stink eye, and Binnie proceeded back to Marshall. Sizing him up, she arched her back and placed her palms on his shoulders.

"Wowza," Marshall said. Carolyn nudged him irritably, but he was entranced.

Suddenly a second figure entered the room, a man wearing a tux. He had both arms raised slightly and was making odd circular jerking gestures with his hands close together. It was…bizarre and slightly unnerving for Rueben to watch.

"Webber?" Martha said.

"Who?" Rueben said.

"The tiki bar bartender."

He had no clue what that was all about but at least the robotic hand motions now made sense. Webber was trying to wipe out a nonexistent glass instead of doing something dirty.

"But what are they doing here…" Rueben mused as Webber stopped "wiping his glass" and picked up a marble rolling pin sitting on the counter. Rueben turned in time to see Binnie slide a chef's knife out from a knife block near her waist. His eyes widened in horror. "It's a trap!"

Binnie spun and sliced at Rueben's chest but he quick-stepped away from her, a move he'd perfected during his ballroom dancing days. As fast as he'd been though, the knife had nicked his shirt and drawn a thin scratch of blood.

Binnie went down in a sexy crouch and was about to leap upward at Rueben with the knife when Aki slammed a cast iron pan against the back of Binnie's head. The sexbot crumpled like a sack of potatoes.

Rueben drew a quick breath. "Thanks."

Buzz wasn't so lucky. Webber swung the marble rolling pin down at him, and Buzz raised his arm in defense. It didn't break, but Buzz cried out in a voice probably loud enough for Rueben-Z to hear, wherever he was.

"I'll decommission you for that," he gasped.

Webber smiled mischievously. "What would you like to drink?"

"Drink this." Marshall closed his meaty hands around the stainless steel prep table. With a grunt, he shoved it forward. Its wheels made a screeching sound as it crashed into Webber at the waist.

"Ow. Would you like a drink?"

Marshall hobbled up to the prep table and put his back into it as he smashed Webber up against the wall with a *crunch*. Webber's torso collapsed onto the prep table.

"Would you like a drink? Would you like a drink?"

"Leave him, let's go," Buzz said, nursing his aching arm.

They followed Buzz out into a hallway, and Buzz stopped in his tracks as Rueben-Z stepped out of a doorway at the far end.

Rueben caught Buzz on the shoulder.

"Ow, man."

Rueben grabbed Buzz's other shoulder instead. "I know this part of the mansion. You take everyone else. I'll buy us some time."

The urgency in Buzz's eyes was painful. "We don't have much time."

Rueben knew what he meant. The plan… He gripped his friend's shoulder and chuckled. "Just don't leave without me. I'll meet you there. Trust me."

"You could die," Martha said. "I thought you weren't going to do any warping until we knew more about the phenomenon."

Rueben smirked. "I've done my fair share of dying in this mansion, training for the Pout mission. I'm not going to die again."

Aki, now standing beside Rueben, bit her lip. "I'll stay with you."

"Stay and die," Rueben-Z taunted from the end of the hallway as he popped his knuckles.

Rueben shook his head. "I know him. I know how he thinks. I'll be safe. I'm not going to die." He embraced her, and she hugged him back tightly. He thought she might have choked back a tear as she did so. Probably not though. She was a badass special agent.

"You better not die." She leaned in and kissed him quick on the lips.

Hell no, I'm not gonna die. Not after that, Rueben thought as his friends and parents started off in the opposite direction. With his heart hammering with excitement, Rueben faced Rueben-Z and called, "Try to keep up!"

He really hadn't thought this plan through. Rueben was taking the stairs two at a time, and he was already starting to get winded. The only thing keeping him going was Aki's kiss.

Man, he really needed to start running more. Behind him, Rueben-Z surprisingly didn't try to roast him with the flamethrower. Did he know that Rueben was running out of steam? Was he just toying with him?

"How did you like my reprogramed version of Buzz's Binnie and Webber?"

Rueben made it to the top of the steps. Up ahead were the ornate oak doors with the bronze lion doorknobs. "We took care of them."

"Ooh, you killed them? You're turning to the dark side rather quickly."

Rueben threw open one of the doors to the theater and dashed inside. By the time Rueben-Z had entered, Rueben was already midway through a row of seats, working his way to the exit on the other side.

"You know," Rueben-Z said, "they say life is a stage—"

"Cut the bullshit. My friends might think you're beyond saving, but I still believe in you."

Rueben-Z pursued Rueben through the rows of seats, gaining on him. It was a rather wide home theater. "You believe in me? Hah. As Marshall would say, cry me a river."

That's it, Rueben thought as Rueben-Z closed in on him. The door was close, but the theater seats were slowing him down in his fatigued state. *Play to his emotions...*

"Of course," Rueben called out loudly over his shoulder. "Maybe they're right. How many worlds have you murdered? You must be the most cold-hearted bastard in existence—"

There was a roar of fury behind Rueben. "I am not to blame! I am trying to fix things!"

Flames *whooshed* up behind Rueben as he reached the end of the row. Gulping in air, he dove and scrambled to his feet for the side door as Rueben-Z spun in a slow half-circle, incinerating the theater around him. "It's not my fault," he was still shouting as Rueben made his way out and back down the steps to the ground floor.

He wasted no time in scampering breathlessly to Buzz's hangar on the other side of the building. He was panting quite heavily when he reached it and was glad to see a dual-rotor jet-copter beside the open, massive hangar door.

One of the jet-copter's doors was open, and his friends and parents were already inside and buckled in. Buzz was hanging out through the jet-copter's door and waving him onward. "Get to the chopper!"

Rueben felt like puking as he clambered up inside. Buzz closed the door and climbed into the cockpit. Even as Rueben struggled to harness himself in, the jet-copter was already out the hangar door and rising steadily.

Marshall nudged him from one side. "Your friend Buzz is an all-right guy."

Rueben nodded, taking quick breaths to try to recover.

On his other side, Aki said, "You did good. I never doubted you." She kissed him.

Martha grinned and shouted over the engine, "Rosa got the goat and monkey out of the conservatory."

Suddenly Buzz's voice came over the jet-copter's intercom. "Okay, everyone take a look out the window behind us."

Buzz pulled a remote from his bathrobe's pocket and raised it dramatically. Then he pushed a button, and fire erupted from inside the mansion far below them. The building exploded into a gigantic fireball, painting the night sky in orange, red, and yellow.

"If we're lucky," Buzz said, "Rueben-Z will think we died in the blast. If we're really lucky, he died."

Rueben shook his head. "I don't think we're that lucky."

"If he did die," Carolyn said, "we are definitely not lucky. He's the cure to the time disease, remember?"

Rueben leaned back against his seat. "Guess we'll have to wait and see."

Marshall grunted. "Waiting to see if a time virus-infected psychopath survived a bomb blast... Kinda reminds me of waiting for a colonoscopy result."

Maybe Rueben-Z got out, and perhaps he didn't. Exhausted as he was, Rueben no longer cared at the moment. He rested his head back, and soon he was asleep.

CHAPTER NINE

Rueben woke to the smell of coffee. It took him a moment to remember where he was, and for a few minutes, all he saw was the wooden base of a bottom bunk. Then it came back to him. He was resting in the bunkroom of Buzz's underground lair.

The Bat Cave.

He seriously had to name it that.

Aside from the authentic stone walls, the spartan room had black concrete floors and three wooden bunk beds installed against the walls. There was a tiny bathroom at one end.

Across from him, Marshall was silent in slumber, thank God for that. Rueben always appreciated the rare moments when Marshall's mouth was closed. He almost looked peaceful. In the bunk above his dad was Carolyn. He hoped things worked out well between his parents once this was all over with.

Maybe then he could get a place for himself and not have

to worry about leaving Marshall alone. Or better yet, perhaps he and Aki could get one together. *Take it slow, Rueben,* he reminded himself. He smelled Aki's perfume in the bunk above him, and his heart quickened.

Martha slept in the remaining bottom bunk with her dark hair splayed across a pillow. The spot above Martha's bed was empty. Buzz hadn't stayed in here. He'd stayed in the luxurious master suite at the end of the hall.

The Bat Cave was underground at some very private property Buzz owned in the Catskill Mountains, and they'd flown here directly after Buzz blew up his mansion. RIP mansion. Buzz, oddly enough, didn't seem too bothered by that now. They still didn't know if they'd caught Rueben-Z in the blast or if he'd escaped, but Rueben figured he probably made it out alive. The villain always did.

In any case, Rueben had never been this far upstate, and the clean mountain air and wide-open spaces were quite unsettling to him. It had taken Martha streaming ambient city noise off her phone for any of them to get any sleep in the silent underground bunk room at first. Rachel, his ex-fiancée, had once mentioned hiking up in these mountains, but the appeal for Rueben had been right up there with root canals and colonoscopies.

Apologies to Tim McGraw, but Rocky Mountain climbing —or any other mountain adventure, for that matter—did not sound like a way to live like one was dying. It sounded more like a way to get mauled by a cougar or slip and break one's leg, and with no medical facilities nearby...

No thanks.

Still, here he was.

The view on the flight over here had been quite stunning:

lots of rolling mountains and grassy peaks dotted with mountain streams.

"So why do you have a secret lair?" Rueben had asked.

Buzz had smiled, and the aircraft had dipped low. For a man that lived for the laws of physics, Buzz sure was a shitty driver and a worse pilot. He winked. "Wouldn't you have one if you could?"

"So you have a secret lair for the hell of it?"

"Pretty much, yeah."

"Well, I guess I can't argue with that logic."

"Plus, you know, chicks dig it if you have a secret lair."

"Really? How'd that work out for Hannibal Lecter?"

"Ah, come on, man. You know that hurts. Why do you have to do that?"

Rueben had laughed, and Buzz had frowned. Then he'd had to pull the aircraft out of a nosedive. When they finally made it to Buzz's private landing strip complete with two fully gassed-up Jeeps, Rueben had never been so glad. That was promptly followed by a harrowing Jeep trip through the mountains and a descent through a trapdoor, down an endless flight of stairs.

They were so exhausted that they'd basically only rested for the rest of Tuesday. Buzz had mentioned that the Bat Cave had several amenities and showed them a map, but they hadn't explored.

For the moment, all they had were the dirty clothes on their backs—a swimsuit in Aki's case, and a swimsuit and bathrobe for Martha—but Buzz said he'd sent Rosa to grab some clothes for them. He had some spare outfits here for himself but not much beyond that. In the meantime, they'd all tended to their wounds and got cleaned up. Aki had bandaged

Rueben up from Hacked Binnie's knife attack. They'd all gone to bed early.

Now, it was morning. Rueben sat up in his bunk and hit his head on the top, and the wood *thudded* against his skull. Above him, Aki gently stirred. She peered down below, and he saw her smile. God, she looked beautiful in the morning, her dark hair tousled, and her bare face natural and raw against the low lamplight coming in from the adjacent bathroom.

She leaned her head on her palm and whispered, "Hey there."

Yeah, maybe Buzz was onto something about the whole chicks and secret lairs thing. Rueben climbed out and leaned against her bunk. "So, how's this for a night out?"

She laughed softly. "I can honestly say that this is the most unique date I've ever been on."

"You know, some guys do dinner and a movie...I thought I'd mix it up a bit."

She winked and tossed her legs over the ladder. "Rueben Peet, no one could ever accuse you of being ordinary." He laughed, and she sat up, and her head *bonked* against the ceiling. "Geez, what did Buzz design this place for?"

From the darkness, Marshall muttered, "Would you two just fuck and get it over with so the rest of us could get some sleep?"

Rueben blushed and rubbed his face, and Aki rolled her eyes and descended the ladder. They both stumbled out of the bunk room and into a large living area.

The living room had orange-and-purple couches, lava lamps on end tables, and gothic sconce lighting on the walls. A large television hung above an electric fireplace. A large round oak table occupied one end of the room, and Buzz sat in a chair in his silk robe, pajamas, and slippers, engrossed in a tablet over his morning coffee and toast.

Rueben rubbed his arms. With the concrete floor and being who only knew how far underground, the fireplace was necessary. He sat on the hearth and warmed his hands. Aki joined him, and for a moment it was only the two of them and the gentle heat.

A blandly mechanical and yet female-looking robot waddled into the room, sweeping the floor with a broom. She was taller and more barrel-chested than Rosa, and instead of looking human like Binnie and Webber, she kind of resembled the robot maid on *The Jetsons*.

She had a sort of rectangular head with glowing lights for eyes, and her skin was all silver and metal. She was flat-chested with a digital screen on her front, and she had blonde pigtails. Rueben liked Binnie better. As soon as the robot sensed Rueben and Aki standing there, it stopped, turned toward them, and asked in a monotone, "Would you like coffee and toast?"

Aki and Rueben stared at each other open-mouthed, and Rueben rubbed the back of his head. "Sure. Why not?"

Aki piped up, "I'd like a soy macchiato with extra foam."

Rueben looked at her. "What do you think this is, Starbucks?"

Aki gave him a sly smile. "You think Buzz programmed a robot that can't make a good cup of coffee?"

"You do have a point there."

"I'm sure she's a damn good bartender too."

The robot left the room, and Buzz casually looked up from his tablet. "She is quite the bartender, I will say."

Rueben and Aki joined Buzz at the table. "What's this robot's name?" Rueben asked.

"That's Emma. She's from my kitchen staff line. I hope to have her commercially viable within five years."

"You have a kitchen line?"

"Oh, I have much more than that."

"What happened to Rosa?"

"I'm not at liberty to say."

Rueben and Aki stared at each other blankly.

"She is getting us clothes, right?" Aki said.

"Yes."

Rueben looked at Buzz. "Do you have any other hideouts like this one?"

"Oh, several. That's all you need to know."

Rueben didn't see the point in asking any more questions. He figured he'd never get to the end of who Buzz was or what he was up to.

Martha, Marshall, and Carolyn stumbled out now, all folding their arms in the cold. Marshall and Carolyn stood off at the back of the group and didn't seem to want to engage with anyone besides each other.

Buzz set down his coffee. "Good morning, everyone. I trust the accommodations were satisfactory. Did we all sleep well?"

Emma soon arrived with Aki's soy macchiato and a black coffee and bland toast for Rueben.

Aki sipped her macchiato and whistled. "This is good."

Rueben spooned sugar into his coffee. "This is what I get for being nice to the robot."

Marshall slapped him on the back. "That's why nice guys finish last."

"Yeah? So what's your excuse?"

Everyone chuckled at the banter, even Marshall, who didn't seem fazed by Emma's presence. "Yeah, Emma, I'd like a black coffee and toast with a slab of butter and jam. And hash browns, if you got them. Not too soft, not too hard, and with just the right amount of grease."

Rueben glanced at Carolyn. They both wondered if Emma's hash browns would be up to Marshall's standards. Martha and Carolyn placed their orders—bagels and coffee—and Emma *beeped* and left the room.

Everyone was quiet now, sitting awkwardly in the living room, and Marshall and Carolyn stepped out what Rueben termed as the cave's "fake" front door. Beyond it was the winding staircase that led up to the trap door. Outside the real front door of the cave was a small quaint sitting area, and Marshall and Carolyn had spent much of last night out there.

Buzz watched them leave. "I guess they have a lot of catching up to do."

Rueben sighed, glad they were getting along better now.

He leaned back into the couch and listened to the sounds of Emma making breakfast. To the side of him, Martha sat at a coffee table. Rueben had mostly recovered from his previous days' exertions, and now he was starting to get bored.

Now what?

Buzz glanced at everyone still inside. "Okay, what are our next steps? Clearly, we need to prepare in case Rueben-Z is still out there. If he survived, he probably wants to kill us even more now that we tried to blow him up."

"He tried to burn us up first," Martha said.

Aki ran her hand through her hair. "Do you think Rueben-Z knows about this hideout?"

Buzz shook his head. "Of course not. This is a safe place for us. No human knows of these contingency bases except for me. I had robots build it, in case you didn't know."

Martha eyed him sharply. "What if Rueben-Z found out about it from a Buzz on a different Earth?"

"Well, that's a possibility, but—"

Aki interjected, "Yeah, I say there's a pretty good chance that Rueben-Z knows all your hideouts no matter how secret you think they are on this Earth."

Buzz looked like he wanted to argue, but then he deflated.

Emma showed up at that point and ejected full plates of everyone's breakfast from her steel abdomen. She laid them all out neatly on the coffee table. All the dishes were steaming hot and looked delicious.

Buzz dismissed her. "Thank you, Emma."

The robot went back into a corner and switched to power-saver mode, and everyone dug into their food as Carolyn and Marshall came back inside and joined them.

Rueben eyed his toast, which was cold by now. He'd been hesitant to try it. Buzz had once given them all a parasite cleanse he'd made in test tubes. It was so bad Rueben couldn't ever forget, but he should have known it'd be disgusting judging by its unnatural neon color.

This toast, however, looked normal. The bread was a healthy burnt color, and the butter and jam looked natural. He took a tentative bite. "Hey, this is quite good."

Aki nodded her agreement over a mouthful of hers.

Marshall took one bite of his hash browns, and his face lit up. He turned to Rueben. "You see, son, this is what hash browns are supposed to taste like."

"Great. So now my cooking skills are backseat to a robot's."

Marshall whistled, and he spoon-fed Carolyn. They laughed together, and Rueben held back nausea. His parents were getting along quite well, it seemed. Marshall held a full fork up to Rueben. "Taste this, come on. Taste how good this is."

Rueben cringed and pushed the fork away. "No thanks. I'll take your word for it."

Marshall passed the fork around the room. "You guys taste this. I mean, this is some good stuff. Buzz, where did she get this recipe?"

Emma spoke in a monotone. "Waffle House."

Marshall snapped his fingers. "That is where it's from." He turned to Carolyn, who nibbled at her bagel. "Do you remember our third date? We went to the Waffle House."

She dropped her bagel. "I do remember that. It was after the Poison concert."

They all laughed, and Aki teased Marshall, "I wouldn't take you for a Poison fan."

He frowned. "You know, if the woman you love—well, to hell with you fuckers. What would any of you know about love?"

Rueben countered, "That every rose has its thorn, that's for sure."

Marshall rolled his eyes at Rueben, and they all laughed. It felt so good.

Buzz cleared his throat. "Emma is a prototype cook robot. She comes preprogrammed with recipes, but she gets smarter over time. She'll pick up restaurants you like from your phone and scan their menus to find suggested menu items, and if available, the recipe itself."

Marshall stared wide-eyed at Emma. "She picked up that I go to Waffle House from my phone?"

"If I looked into her programming and data usage history, I would likely find that's what she did."

Marshall protectively clasped his phone. "What else does she pick up?"

"Just food preferences for now. She's not some type of spy surveillance device. Um, now let's get back to business. We have to figure out what to do about Rueben-Z if he shows up. And also the time disease phenomenon that he most likely brought to this world. We're probably going to need a plan for that."

They all agreed. After they finished eating, of course.

CHAPTER TEN

<u>**Wednesday, May 24, 11:11 a.m.**</u>

Buzz led everyone into a conference room with a white dry-erase board at the front and waited for everyone to take their seats. "Let's take it from the top, shall we? Emma, a round of drinks for everyone."

Martha held up a hand. "How about we make that water instead of booze?"

"What?" Buzz said, but everyone else agreed with Martha.

After ordering a beer, Buzz began. "I think first we ought to rewind to the mansion. While I am still grieving over its destruction…the loss wasn't total."

"We all saw it explode when we were on the jet-copter," Martha said. "It was dark outside, but I'm pretty sure that was a total loss."

Buzz sighed. "What I mean to say is I'm not totally without computer resources. Basically, I backed up all my data to the cloud. However, I am short of some computing power here in this place."

Marshall spoke up. "Are you saying the Internet might be a

bit slow here?" Buzz nodded. "Then why didn't you just say that?"

Before Buzz could respond, Rueben said, "Do you know if Rueben-Z made it out of the blast?"

"Ah yes." Buzz tapped his fingertips on the desk in front of him. "I managed to pull up security footage from the mansion right before it exploded. Rueben-Z did make it out beforehand. As for now, he's in the wind. With him still being alive, that means the time virus threat is still very real."

"What about those two lumberjack robots?" Aki added. "Do you think they made it out as well?"

Buzz laughed. "Those two 'lumberjack robots' are most certainly dead. They're so dumb they were probably still bashing up my server room when the explosion went off. Now, moving on—"

Martha raised her hand. "Wait, I have a question."

"Yes?"

"I understand why someone like you would build sexbots —I mean robots—like Binnie. Why'd you ever make lumber-jack-themed robots? There something you want to tell us?"

Buzz's face flushed. "That's not relevant—"

"Inquiring minds want to know." Martha smirked.

"I was curious about that myself," Aki said.

"Fine. Fine. If you must know, I went through a stage in my childhood when I wanted to grow up and be strong like a lumberjack someday, okay? Jeez. Gimme a break. I was, like, twelve when I designed their schematics. Now, can we please move on to the important stuff?"

They discussed everything they knew about Rueben-Z and listened as Carolyn made a list and recounted what she and Rueben-Z had tried to stop the virus on the other worlds. Eventually, they all grew restless.

Everyone was thinking the same thing, but Marshall said it first. "I need a break."

Everyone agreed except for Buzz. He disappeared into a triumvirate of laptop screens. Marshall turned to Martha. "Billiards? I spotted that on the map."

She laughed. "Not unless you want your ass kicked like the last time we played a few years back."

"Well, I'm a gentleman. I didn't want to embarrass a lady."

"Is that right? So you threw the game against a younger, rookie officer?"

"When you put it that way, it's game on."

They both smirked and slipped off into an adjacent room.

Rueben watched them leave, and Aki rolled her eyes. "They sure get along like a father and a daughter. Just watching them, I kind of feel left out."

Rueben was glad that Martha was there to help keep Marshall in line although Carolyn seemed to be doing a good job of that as well now. He sighed and turned to Aki. "You know what I'd love to do once this is all over?"

"What?"

"I'd like to take you out, properly. You know, like to a restaurant or Shakespeare in the Park, like what normal couples do. And have normal conversations that don't involve 'resetting' or psychotic villains."

She smiled and played with his hair. "I'd like that. I'd like that very much although fighting Rueben-Z and his minions at the mansion alongside you was pretty good too. All the adrenaline and danger and all that."

He looked into her deep brown eyes, and his heart raced. He felt like he could sit there all night with her, staring into her eyes.

She told him, "I have an idea."

"Oh yeah?"

She toyed with his hand and brought it to her lips. "Let's go to the hot spring."

He raised an eyebrow. "The hot spring?"

"Yeah. We can be like a normal couple and pretend we're on vacation."

"Instead of in an underground lair plotting how to stop a parallel future version of myself from inadvertently destroying the world with a time virus?"

"Yeah, all that." She whispered hotly into his ear, "Let's just be you and me."

He smiled at the idea, then rose and followed Aki down a long, narrow hallway, going deeper into the earth. They arrived at a metal door, and she opened it.

Overpowering humidity and the sound of rushing water immediately greeted them. Rueben's mouth dropped. It was a real mountain cave with walls an aged yellow and orange color. About ten feet up, a wide waterfall cascaded down into the cave and circulated in and out of a small pool. Steam rose from the water in a fine mist.

Aki winked at him and stepped into the pool one shapely, sexy foot at a time. "You coming?"

He couldn't take his eyes off her. "Uh, yeah." In a flash, he slipped off his shirt and jeans and got down to his black boxers. "How hot is it?"

"Not too bad. It feels like a hot tub, really."

She waded in, waist-deep now, and he followed her. She was right. It felt like a sauna. He watched as she leaned back and wet her hair, marveling at how it fell in short, wet strands around her face. The steam rose around her, and it looked like the fog in a hot beach ad.

He couldn't believe he was in this scene. Usually, the guys in the ads were finely chiseled, with rock-hard abs and striking smiles, or eyes that looked unnaturally blue. He was an average guy. He was skinny and lanky overall, and he didn't have that surging confidence to knock a woman off her feet. He was always too worried about saying the wrong thing to ever really say the right one and usually erred on the side of caution by not offending them.

Maybe he had always been too cautious. Perhaps he should risk more. Maybe he should be that guy in the Calvin Klein ad. What would that guy do? With slow, dramatic arm strokes, Rueben swam up behind her. Then he kissed the back of her shoulders. To his shock, she let him. He grabbed her and pulled her toward him, kissing the back of her neck the whole time. She leaned into his kisses.

"Hey you two, get a room!"

They both started at Buzz's voice. He came out in his swim shorts, holding a cocktail. Rueben softly groaned and released Aki, and Buzz entered the pool. "I think we're all a little over-worked. Some relaxation in this hot spring would be good for us all."

Aki swam to the side of the pool and glanced upward. "You know what you should invent, Buzz? A massage therapist robot."

He made a face. "They never do what you want them to do."

Rueben joined Aki against the side of the pool, and the three of them sat with the water up to their shoulders, enjoying the steam and warmth. Buzz sipped his drink.

"What's on your mind, buddy?" Buzz asked.

Rueben tried to relax the tension in his shoulders and neck. "This time disease my mom told us about. I'm worried. About this Earth. The way it devastated all those other worlds…"

Aki laid her hand on his wrist. "We'll figure it out. We've got Buzz."

Buzz did a half-bow. "Why, thank you."

"Yeah," Rueben said, "but he couldn't stop the phenomenon on any of the other worlds. That's what worries me so much. This isn't some kind of physical opponent we can punch and kick and shoot. I kind of miss the days of Pout and Pete."

Silence fell over the cavern as they all grappled with the idea of the time disease.

Martha entered the cave, wearing her robe. She'd wrapped her long, dark hair in a high bun and carried a beer. "Who died?"

Rueben sighed. "The whole world if we don't find a way to stop the time disease from taking hold on this Earth."

Martha dipped her toes into the water. "Oh. That." She opted to sit on the side of the hot spring beside them, with her feet dangling in the water. "I'm glad I'm finally using my vacation days. Use 'em or lose 'em, as the other cops say." They all chuckled, but it was a nervous sound.

Carolyn showed up then, her outfit from the day before smudged and wrinkled. "Hi, guys. Mind if I join you?"

Buzz toasted Carolyn with his cocktail. "Be our guest."

She sat beside everyone else and followed Martha's lead by only putting her feet in.

Buzz included her in the conversation. "We're trying to figure out how to stop the world from ending. You know, the usual."

She didn't respond. She just stared thoughtfully into the water.

Marshall was the last to arrive, holding a folding chair and a beer. "You're all just hanging out with your dicks...and vaginas in your hands. We got Rueben-Z out there doing God knows what. Let's work on this."

Buzz greeted him. "Hey, Marshall. You weren't here, so you know, nothing got done."

They all laughed, and Marshall raised an eyebrow and chuckled. "Sounds about right."

He unfolded his chair and plopped down in it. Then, turning to the side, Marshall rested the lip of his beer bottle against the rocky ridges of the cave's wall and popped off the cap with a well-placed smack of his palm. He smiled and took a long gulp.

Martha turned to Carolyn. "Anything else you can tell us? Something that might help us figure this out?"

Carolyn shook her head.

"Come on," Martha pressed. "There's got to be something."

"This is your home and where all of you belong. You'll do anything to save it. The other Earth was mine. I've never felt really at home since. Well, except for those ten years..."

Her words trailed off, and Rueben and Marshall caught her meaning. They both shifted uneasily.

Buzz snapped his fingers. "Carolyn, roughly how long were you and Rueben-Z on the other Earths before the time disease triggered?"

Carolyn dipped her hand into the hot water and watched the ripples. "It varied, really. A few days. A few months. We were on one world for over a year before...before *it* came and destroyed it."

"Okay. But there has to be some kind of variable that triggered the phenomenon. Think, Carolyn, think."

"I am thinking. I am…"

Rueben leaned forward. "Mom? What is it?"

"Maybe nothing. Rueben-Z…when we first started hopping to other Earths, we didn't warp much once we arrived. We were trying to get a feel for life in a world parallel to ours. We kept to ourselves. Settled in a new city. Didn't interact with the parallel versions of the people we had known on Earth-Z. People we had watched crumble to dust, helpless to do anything to stop it."

Rueben couldn't imagine the pain of watching his friends die that way right in front of him.

"Together, we sought out all the top physicists around the country. Although a few believed us, most just laughed at us. Each time either Rueben-Z or I would kill ourselves and warp back to before we had told them and seek out the next one. Deep down, we knew that that world's Buzz was probably the only scientist with the ability to save Earth-Z.

"We reached out to Buzz, and he ran all kinds of tests and experiments on our warping abilities. He was able to view videos and information on all of Rueben-Z's previous deaths and warps via the nanobot in his body that Buzz-Z had injected into him."

Carolyn sighed. "It wasn't long until one day the phenomenon struck, right there in Buzz's lab. Buzz withered away right in front of us. Turned to dust. Horrified, we ran outside and saw that the grass around the mansion had already died and was continuing to die in an ever-expanding circle. Bugs, birds, rabbits, plants, people. All were in the phenomenon's expanding radius. All turned to dust. Except us."

Back in the hot spring room, everyone looked devastated, like they were going to be sick.

Carolyn continued. "There isn't much more to say. We warped back to before Buzz had died. We told him what had happened. He ran some tests and died before us again in the same way. We warped back even farther the next time, and the phenomenon struck again—sooner this time. Eventually, we climbed back into the space and time capsule and hopped to another parallel world. To try to find a way to stop it."

For a time, no one could find any words to say.

Then Buzz said, "I will add all this to my Rules for Repeaters. *The time virus seems to go inactive when the infected Repeater hops to a parallel Earth. After a certain passage of time, the virus reactivates.*" Buzz paused. "*Warping may speed up the virus's activation and cause it to go airborne and destroy the Earth eventually.*" Buzz turned to Carolyn. "How long has Rueben-Z been on Earth-A?"

Rueben glanced at his friends. "Long enough for him to ingratiate himself with Pout."

Buzz thumbed his chin. "So he's been here at least a few months. And the time disease hasn't struck yet. How many times has Rueben-Z warped backward on this Earth?"

"There's no way to tell," Carolyn said.

Aki's eyes widened. "Now that he can't warp anymore, maybe the time disease will stay dormant?"

Martha shook her head. "I doubt things will be that easy for us."

CHAPTER ELEVEN

Wednesday, May 24, 3:04 p.m.

They all took turns showering after leaving the hot spring while Buzz returned to the conference room to review his notes.

Rueben was thinking about Buzz's notes, trying to make heads or tails of them, when Aki came out of the shower with a towel wrapped turban-style around her head. "Your turn."

Great. A shower would be a nice distraction. He was heading to the bathroom when Aki called to him. He turned with a quizzical look, and she handed him a shopping bag full of clothing. "Thought you might want these."

He took the clothing. "Um, thanks?"

She laughed. "Rosa finally showed up. I guess clothes shopping for all of us took a long time."

"I hope she didn't shop at Old Navy."

Aki laughed again. "I think I saw a Hawaiian shirt in there."

He met Aki's eyes. The way she looked at him, he wanted so badly to pick up where they had left off in the hot spring.

She looked away. "Well, I'll let you get back to it."

"Yeah. Well, thanks for bringing the clothes."

"No problem."

She left, and he went into the bathroom to shower. He was in love with her—definitely more in love than he'd ever been with Rachel. Did she feel the same way about him? He turned on the water.

When Rueben got out of the shower, the conference room had transformed into a war room. Several whiteboards and easels full of Buzz's hasty scribbles were stationed throughout the room, detailing "Operation Z."

"What the..." Rueben's words trailed off as he spotted multiple computer workstations, each with two monitors and a laptop. Aki sat at one station and Martha and Carolyn sat at two across the room. On the table closest to the door was a computer printout with everyone's names and their "current assignment." Rueben scanned the page and found his name. Buzz had tasked him and Aki with using CIA resources to find Rueben-Z's current location.

That didn't sound too difficult. He sat in front of the laptop next to Aki, already tapping away on her keyboard. She didn't say anything, only gave him a slight smile as she stared into her screen. He was surprised when her sock-covered toe rubbed his up and down. He grinned and reciprocated the gesture while he logged into the online CIA portal.

Across from them, Carolyn frowned into her screen. She wore reading glasses, and Rueben reluctantly admitted that the glasses added a homey-ness that made her look maternal.

Rueben turned back to his workstation and started using the CIA's resources to search NYC for signs of Rueben-Z. Aki had already cleared her and Rueben's absence from the CIA so the roster listed them as "on assignment."

Sometime later, Buzz walked in with a tiny circuit board. He sat at a spot near the front of the room and began to tinker with it.

"What are you working on?" Rueben finally asked.

"Something that might help us."

"Cryptic much?" Aki smiled.

"It's…far from finished. But it's good to keep my hands moving. Helps me think."

Rueben could understand that. He worked at his laptop for a few hours until his eyes needed a break and his legs needed stretching. He leaned over and checked out what Aki was doing. She had a possible sighting of Rueben-Z at a clothing store. She told him to stretch his legs without her so Rueben got up and ambled out of the room.

He heard the low hum of classic rock music coming down the halls, and he followed it to the billiard room where his father was playing pool by himself.

He glanced up at Rueben. "Had enough of that computer nerd bullshit in there?"

"Dad. You can cut the act. Mom told me all about how you used to be in the computer science field before you went into law enforcement."

Marshall appeared to have a comeback, but he thought better of it and shrugged. He handed Rueben his cue stick and nodded at the pool table.

Rueben leaned over, lined up a shot, and sent a ball swirling into a corner pocket.

"Good job, son. Your technique was shit, but you got it in there."

"Thanks."

Marshall eyed him soberly with one hand resting on the pool table. "Look, son, I know I've been a hardass to you nearly all your life. Well, after your mom left. And there ain't no cause for it. I guess I lost track of what mattered. Grew into a mean old man."

"Dad, you're forty-five."

Marshall sighed and slapped a hand against his gut. "Feels much older when you don't take care of yourself."

"It's never too late to start, is it?"

Marshall chuckled. "Your optimism reminds me of your mother." He paused and drew a heavy breath. "I never wanted any of this for you. I hoped you wouldn't get that time-warping gene or whatever it is like your mother."

Rueben nodded.

"I knew it was a possibility you'd be like her when you grew up, but I wasn't going to let it run your life like it did hers. I'd hoped you would have a long, long, happy life before you got mixed up in all of this. Maybe settled down with that girl Aki. Maybe died of old age.

"This power, it's like a curse. Or, a reference you might get, it's like what's his name, Spiderman's uncle tells him. 'With great power comes great responsibility' and all that bullshit. Well, it's true, and I don't envy you and your mother for what you can do. I don't know if I'd be strong enough to…" Marshall's words choked off, and he cleared his throat.

Rueben reached out and patted his father's arm. "It's okay, Dad. It's all okay. I haven't exactly been the best son either, although I do try."

Marshall tensed. "You know, your hash browns aren't as bad as I make 'em out to be," he said quietly.

"What?" Rueben said.

Marshall loudly cleared his throat again and shook his

head in a manly sort of way. "Uh, I said I appreciate all you do for me. Food, meds. That stuff. You do a lot for me. And how do I thank you? By drinking too much and turning the TV up. By pushing you farther out of my life each day—"

"Dad." Rueben clapped a hand on Marshall's shoulder.

Marshall shrugged it off. "No. I'm not done. You know those mugs that say 'World's Best Dad?'"

Rueben nodded.

"Well, you gave me one when you were eight for Father's Day. I mean, Carolyn bought it and wrapped it and you probably signed the card, but it meant a lot to me at the time. I never used it for fear I'd chip it, but it meant the world to me, and I kept it on my dresser so I'd see it every day when I got up." He paused heavily. "After your mom left and I fell apart, I tucked the mug away in the cupboard, too ashamed to even look at it. Because truth is, I'm the world's most irredeemable asshole."

"That's not true."

"It is. Your mom's leaving made me weak."

An idea came to Rueben. "I don't think it was just Mom."

Marshall's face was a contorted mess of anguish. It eased up for a moment as he turned to his son. "Huh?"

"Thorne."

Marshall's face paled a shade, and he stammered. "Th-Thorne? What's he got to do with anything?"

"What you did," Rueben said. "When he hijacked the bus, and you came and rescued me and the other kids. Then Thorne escaped and ran off into the woods, and you went in after him and followed..."

Marshall's shoulders rolled forward, and he huffed out a sad sob.

Rueben watched as his father tried to fight becoming a

soggy mess. "I think you think you're a bad person for what you did. But I don't think so. I'm not sure how it all went down in the woods, and I don't need to know. What you did was beyond loving, and I think it really messed you up inside."

"The coroner," Marshall began, "the coroner said it wasn't my shot that killed him but trauma from the bus crash. He'd hit his head or some shit. He was good as dead regardless of if I'd shot him. But I did shoot him. I shot him in the back as he ran. Because he wouldn't leave my family alone.

"You didn't see Carolyn back then. She was barely keeping it together. And there was you to look after. I thought once Thorne was gone the world would go back to normal. Hell… son, I ain't never told anyone this stuff. It feels good. Like I'm lighter or something. Maybe I shoulda went to the shrink to get checked out afterward. I don't know. But…" He met Rueben's eyes. "Thanks."

Rueben smiled and nodded, and Marshall ran a meaty hand through Rueben's head as if tousling a child's hair. Rueben laughed and so did Marshall, wiping away a tear.

Marshall now stood a little taller than he had in years, his shoulders thrust back proudly. Rueben beamed, feeling a bit lighter himself. Now, with his eyes rested and his legs adequately stretched, it was time to go back to the conference room and get back to work.

CHAPTER TWELVE

<u>**Wednesday, May 24, 7:08 p.m.**</u>

Martha sat at her workstation, going blind as she stared at her screens. On the force, she never had to be on a computer for this long. She went on patrols, which often involved writing citations, making arrests, and occasionally chasing down criminals.

This was pure torture.

She'd spent the last several hours going through New York police reports in the hopes of running down a lead on Rueben-Z. After Aki had found blurry security camera footage of him in the city, they had worked together and found the hotel Rueben-Z was staying at. He'd paid over the phone in advance with one of Rueben's credit cards.

How he got the card information, they didn't know, but Rueben-Z might have snuck into Rueben's and Marshall's place back before the Pout mission and written it down in case he needed some quick cash. Now maybe he was trying to anger Rueben or flush him out into the open by using his credit card.

No matter the reason, they now had a rough location for Rueben-Z. The only problem was, it might very well be a trap for them.

Martha and Aki both had security footage pulled up on their computers, but the footage they really needed was from the pawnshop across from the hotel. The problem was, it was closed circuit, and there was no way to hack into it from any computer.

Using a phone app on her laptop, Martha called her partner Jake at the precinct. After solving the Pout case, she had some clout at the precinct, and she was able to get Jake to order an officer over to the pawnshop to get a copy of the security footage. She told him it might be a lead on a perp she was tracking down in her free time. He told her that she ought to relax on her time off, and she thanked him and said she'd be around to pick it up sometime.

Martha hung up and turned to Aki. "Rueben not back yet?"

"Nope. His legs must really have needed stretching. Maybe he got lost."

They both giggled, then their tired eyes met, and they said in unison, "Drink time?"

They laughed again. Martha was beginning to see what Rueben saw in Aki. She was a fun person to hang around with, and she was capable at her job.

Aki glanced over at Buzz, still tinkering with some type of circuit board. "Hey Buzz, where's the nearest bar?"

Buzz grinned. "One moment ladies, and I'll show you the most relaxing room in this whole place."

Martha and Aki exchanged a glance. Then Buzz rose from his work. "Follow."

He led them down a long hallway. The lair was a maze. When Martha first got here, she thought it was just the bunk room, the living room, Buzz's room, and a bathroom. Then she'd discovered the hot spring and the billiard room. This place was practically an underground mansion carved out of stone.

Buzz took them farther into the earth, the sconced lighting along the tunnel hallways occasionally flickering. She winced. She wasn't sure if she liked being so deep in the ground with iffy lighting.

Buzz remarked, "The lighting is intentional. In imitation of flickering torchlight. Don't worry. The electricity down here is flawless."

Aki noted, "I would think you'd be off the grid here."

"We are. It's a natural energy recycling system that runs off groundwater. I have a mini private power plant above ground."

They went deeper and deeper down a few more hallways, and eventually, he flipped open a set of fancy gold doors.

He ceremoniously announced, "The massage room."

Paintings of tranquil nature scenes hung on the cave walls, and dark red leather couches and beds abounded. There were even a couple of padded massage tables where you laid down, with a cutout for your head. There was also a small unobtrusive table with a remote control on it and some tanning beds off to one side. One of them showed lights as if it was in use.

Aki asked him, "Is someone in there?"

He winked. "Not just anyone." He clapped his hands. "Biddie."

The top part of the tanning bed opened, and out climbed the most beautiful woman Martha had seen in a while. Her mouth dropped. She was tall and blond and wore black short-shorts and a black halter that showed off the biggest boobs she had seen in person. She had really tan skin and wasn't wearing any eye protection or the proper clothes for tanning. "Good afternoon, Buzz. I missed you. Where have you been?"

He winked. "Wouldn't you like to know?"

She laughed and ran her palm along his arm. "You're so cute. Isn't he just the cutest?"

Martha and Aki glanced at each other. "There's no way to answer that."

Buzz blushed. "I want you to take extra-special care of my friends, Martha and Aki, here. They're VIP guests, all right?"

Biddie turned to them and pursed her thick lips. "VIP guests, huh? Well, we'll have to set you up right."

Buzz left the room, and Biddie sashayed up to them. She clasped her hands over her heart and told Aki, "I just love your look. I like, want those shoes. Chanel. Yes."

Aki glanced down at the ballet flats she wore. "They are Chanel."

She turned to Martha. "I love your hair. So pretty. How do you get it to do that? What is your secret? Ohhh, can I touch it?"

Martha shrugged. No one had ever gushed over her hair before. "Sure."

Biddie fingered a lock of her hair. "Oh my God, so soft. I just love it. Oh my God, I just love you two. We are going to have so much fun. Now, what can I get you guys to drink? Come on, don't be shy. Buzz has a home gym, so we can work it all off later and just have sooo much fun now."

Martha ordered a beer, and Aki went with an apple martini. When Biddie left, Martha thought she might have a headache from all of Biddie's energy. She asked Aki, "So you don't think she's..."

"Real? Oh God, hell no."

They both laughed.

Martha shrugged. "The compliments were nice, though."

"I think that's the point of her existence. You think she's a massage robot?"

After all the computer work they'd done today, a massage might be just what the doctor ordered.

They kicked off their shoes and sat next to each other on one of the dark red leather couches. They looked more expensive than any of the couches in Buzz's mansion, and when Martha fumbled at the controls on the side to try to recline her section, the entire couch started to vibrate.

Martha facepalmed.

"That feels so good." Aki searched on her side of the couch for any more special features. Martha had to admit that it did feel damn good. She found the recline button, kicked back, and closed her eyes.

Biddie arrived a few minutes later with their drinks and a tray of steaming food. "I brought you guys quesadillas—low-cal, of course. But let Mexican night officially begin. Quesadillas and girl talk."

Martha wondered what the hell time it was. Was it already late? How long had they been staring at computer screens?

Her stomach suddenly grumbled, and she realized she was hungry. But "girl talk?" Martha turned to Aki and saw she had the same expression on her face. "Thanks, Biddie. That'll be enough for now. I was hoping to uh, spend some time alone with Aki."

"Oh, totes. Like, BFF bonding, I just love it." She blew them double-kisses. "No worries. Love you, bitches. I'll catch up with you later. Just holler if you need me."

She started to leave and turned back. "Oh, and if you want to listen to some of Buzz's music, the sound system remote is on that end table. I'll let you in on a secret...it's orgasmic."

Then Biddie left the room, and Martha and Aki burst into laughter. "So bizarre," Aki said.

Martha agreed. "And so different from Binnie."

"Yeah, Binnie was more sultry, and this one is like…"

Martha winced. "Ugh, girls like that get on my nerves."

Aki sipped her drink. "Hey, I used to be a girl like that."

"I won't hold it against you. You're all right in my book."

"Thanks." Aki smiled and tried a bite of her quesadilla. Her eyes rolled back in their sockets. "Wow, these are really good."

Martha tried hers. Aki wasn't kidding. "How did Buzz's robots learn to cook so well?"

Aki swallowed some of her food with her apple martini. "I don't know, but Rueben and I were talking about going on a normal date sometime soon. To tell you the truth, I'd take these robot-prepared quesadillas any time over going to the movies."

Martha paused. "You really like him, don't you?"

Aki cocked her head. "He's interesting. He might look ordinary, but he has so many surprises."

Martha didn't know how to interpret that, and an awkward silence followed. "Music?" She tilted her head at the remote control on the small end table.

"Hells yeah. I can only imagine what kind of tunes Buzz has ready for us."

"It's orgasmic," Martha mimed in a parody of Biddie's voice, and they started laughing again. Martha set her beer to the side, got up, and went over to the table with her quesadilla in her hand.

Right before she reached the end table, a dribble of melted cheese leaked out from her quesadilla, and she bent to wipe it up with her finger. That's when her cop's eyes spotted the button under the table.

"What are you looking at?" Aki asked.

Martha crawled under the table so that she could get a better look. She could barely make out a small black control panel under the table with some words beside it. "It's a button. And the words, 'Make it okay.'"

Aki scrunched up her eyebrows. "What's that supposed to mean?"

"I don't know. Buzz didn't mention anything about it. Think I should push it?"

Aki shrugged and sipped her apple martini.

Martha pushed the button. There was a loud *whoosh,* then nothing. She frowned and returned to her comfy spot on the couch beside Aki. "It didn't do anything."

Aki kicked back her side of the couch and sighed in an exaggerated manner. "I love our little group."

Suddenly Martha felt a wave of sentiment rush through her like adrenaline. "I do too. I love all of you guys. And Marshall is such a sweetie. He acts all tough and sarcastic, but sometimes I want to give him a big hug, you know?"

"Oh, I know," Aki said with a completely straight face. "And Carolyn, such a great mom. I wish my mom was more like her."

"I know, right? She makes the best cookies." Martha's eyes suddenly widened and strangely, she felt like a kid again. "You know what would make this moment even better?"

"What?" Aki said breathlessly.

"Let's ask Biddie to bake us some chocolate chip cookies!" Even though some part of Martha knew that something was very wrong with her body, she was helpless to fight against it. Had she been drugged?

Biddie stepped back into the room. "Can I get you two ladies something else?"

Martha stared at her, trying to fight the chemicals running through her veins or whatever was going on with her. "You know," she said slowly. "Biddie, you're just...so great. Such a sweetheart."

"Oh, thank you, I just love you, too. Both of you guys. Group hug."

The three hugged each other, then suddenly Aki pulled back and shook her head. Desire gleamed in her eyes, and she ran her tongue over her lips. She seemed to be trying to fight the effects too. "I'm not...feeling so...I've gotta go."

Aki started for the door, and Martha called to her, "Wait, where are you going? You're like my best friend, ever."

The door closed behind Aki, and Biddie turned to Martha with a sexy smirk on her face. "Martha, would you like a massage?"

For some reason, Martha liked the way Biddie had said her name. She *really* liked it. The next moment, Martha was holding out her hand, and Biddie was guiding her to one of the padded massage tables.

Biddie's hands were warm and soft as she eased Martha onto the table by the shoulders. "I think you're really going to enjoy this."

"Am I?" Martha heard herself saying. She turned her head back to see where Biddie was. She felt like she was in a blissful, drunken stupor and it felt good. God, it felt so good to cut loose of all the tension.

Behind her, Biddie scooped up the remote control on the end table, and a moment later, the air in the room began to pulse with lush electric dance music.

Oh my God... Was it the massage table that was vibrating or was it her ears?

Biddie was behind her again. Her hands began to massage

Martha's shoulders, working out knots and kinks she didn't even know she had. A moan escaped her as Biddie's hands traveled skillfully down her back.

"Do you want more?" Biddie asked.

The dance music was throbbing through every bone in Martha's body. She felt like she was partying on a cloud with no inhibitions.

"Yes," she groaned.

Biddie cocked her ear. "What was that? Did you say you wanted more?"

"Yes!"

"One moment then." Biddie's hands left Martha's body, and irritated, Martha turned over onto her back. She watched as Biddie moved to the end table and messed with the remote. Soft bedroom music began to seep through unseen speakers.

"Biddie?" Martha said.

Then Biddie tore off her top and hopped up onto the massage table, straddling Martha's thighs. "I think you're really going to enjoy this."

***

The next thing Martha knew, the room was very bright, and she was waking up on the leather couch under a fleece blanket. She had one hell of a headache, and she raised her hands to fend off the ceiling lights. Finally, her eyes focused on the doorway.

"Fuck me…"

Buzz.

He stood there in the doorway with his hands in his pockets. "I see Biddie gave you the full treatment."

Martha's eyes searched the room for her clothes.

"Your shirt's over there." Buzz pointed toward the massage table. "And your pants are…" He jerked his head toward the tanning beds.

"What the fuck happened, you pervert!"

"You pressed the button. I didn't tell you to press the button."

"Button?" She wrapped the blanket around her body and went to retrieve her clothes.

Buzz chuckled. "The oxytocin button beneath the end table."

"Oxytocin?"

"You know. The love hormone—"

"I know what oxytocin is." Martha slipped her shirt back on. "It's what the body produces during sex. So, wait, you put that in the air so people…"

"Will want to have sex, yes."

"So basically this is an oxytocin gas chamber?"

He shrugged. "I like to think of it as my little looove shack."

"I thought it was a massage room."

"The thing about massage therapist robots… They never do what you want them to do. Say, where's Aki?"

Meanwhile, Aki cornered Rueben alone in the bunk bed room and was already completely stripped naked before she even managed to say, "Hello."

CHAPTER THIRTEEN

<u>**Thursday, May 25, 9:32 a.m.**</u>

Rueben drummed his fingers against the tabletop of his workstation in the conference room. He hadn't seen Aki since last night.

Sure, she'd caught him off guard, and it was so crazy. And good. Better than anything he had ever experienced before in his life. Then in the morning, she was gone, and he didn't know what had happened. What did last night mean to her? Nothing?

He loved her. He knew that. He wanted to tell her that but not if he was only a good time for her. He wanted something more with her.

He thought back to last night when she had shown up in front of him with that look in her eyes and…

"For crying out loud," Buzz complained. "We're missing someone. I thought I said morning meeting at nine-thirty a.m."

Buzz, Martha, Marshall, and Carolyn turned to look at Aki's empty seat, then at Rueben. Rueben held up his hands.

"Oh shit," Martha muttered and glared at Buzz, who thrust his hands into his pockets and started to whistle.

Rueben didn't know what that was all about

"Well, find her," Martha said. Buzz picked up a tablet and started flicking through surveillance footage inside the cave.

"Ah yes, she's in the artificial greenhouse." Buzz straightened his shirt collar with a glance Martha's way. "Alone."

Rueben nodded and got up to find Aki. First, though, he grabbed a cup of coffee to take to her.

Rueben didn't know the place had a greenhouse in it. He eventually found it behind a steel reinforced door in what might have been the center of Buzz's lair.

It had a high ceiling with small trees and bushes and grass growing from soil covering the stone floor. There was a fresh humid quality to the place that made him feel like he was out in the woods somewhere instead of below the ground. A few small streams flowed through the room, and insects chirped and buzzed. It reminded him of the conservatory in Buzz's mansion but on a much smaller scale.

Wide rectangular light panels on the ceiling basked the entire area in surprisingly realistic morning "sunshine," and he had to shield his eyes if he looked directly up at it. As he glanced around at the green growth, Rueben wondered how Buzz had the time to take care of any of this stuff, given that all he did was wander around in his slippers, get drunk, and tinker with robots. That was probably the answer right there. Robots.

Stepping lightly upon the soft grass, Rueben followed a

stream to where Aki was sitting at a small bistro table with her laptop. She didn't look up when he approached.

"Brought you a…lukewarm cup of coffee."

She smiled and took the cup. "Thank you. Ah, lukewarm as advertised."

"It was hot. Back when I started the hike to the greenhouse."

"I know, this place is so huge."

"Yeah."

An awkward silence passed between them.

She broke it. "Look, about last night, I…"

He interrupted her. "Aki, I've been meaning to tell you—"

She cut him off. "Let me get this out first. I think I might have been drunk on something. I mean something weird, and my hormones went full-blown crazy. I…just want you to know that wasn't me, and I'm not like that."

Rueben frowned at the bistro table and played with the edge. "Um, okay."

She sipped the coffee, and Rueben tried to read her expression. "So you're not really into me, is that what you're saying? Last night was good, but it was as fake as the sunlight down here?" There was a disappointed tone in his words, but he didn't say them harshly.

"No, no, that's not what I'm saying at all."

"I don't understand. I mean, we had that moment in the hot tub, and I thought it was something."

"It was something," Aki said.

"Look, Aki, I…" He stopped. This was definitely not the time to tell her he loved her.

She placed her hand on his palm. "Rueben, my feelings for you are real."

"Okay."

"It's just I'm still a little confused as to what overcame me last night. Martha and I were hanging out together, and the best I can come up with is Buzz's massage therapist robot spiked me with a massive dose of oxytocin."

It sounded ridiculous, but Rueben didn't laugh. Knowing Buzz, that's probably exactly what had happened to Aki.

"What I'm saying," Aki continued, "is that I didn't want our first time together to be like that. That's all."

Rueben's shoulders relaxed, and he grinned. "Are you saying that you want me to kill myself and warp back so that you won't remember last night…"

She punched him playfully on the arm.

"…because I thought it went pretty well."

She laughed. "You dork. No, you can't warp back. It could interact with the time disease if it's here and you don't want to start the apocalypse, do you?" She paused, her smirk turning incredibly sexy. "You thought last night was that good? You haven't seen anything yet."

Rueben chuckled. "Fine by me. Now I think we ought to head back to the conference room before Buzz sends his massage therapist robot after us both."

Rueben and Aki made it back to the Operation Z meeting in the conference room. Everyone was finishing eating some donuts Emma had brought. Buzz wiped icing and crumbs from his hands. "Come on, people. The fate of the world is in our hands. Let's try to be on time."

Aki smiled apologetically, and she and Rueben took their seats.

Buzz started the meeting. "Here are your assignments:

Rueben, Aki. You both are going to do some surveillance outside the hotel Rueben-Z is supposedly staying at. It's possible that it's a trap. Until we can confirm that he's in there, you are to watch only."

"Sounds easy enough," Aki said.

"And," Buzz continued, "if Rueben-Z does show up, I need you two to get a blood sample from him."

"You expect him just to hand over his blood?" Rueben asked.

Buzz scowled. "You're going to have to use your combat skills and draw it yourself. I'll give you a syringe before you go. Any questions?"

They didn't have any questions.

Next, Buzz turned to Martha and Marshall. "As for you two, you're going to stop by the police precinct to view the pawnshop footage of the hotel from across the street. You did call your partner to get the footage, correct?"

"Yes, oh great one," Martha said jokingly.

"Good. You and Marshall go through the footage and call Rueben and Aki if you come across Rueben-Z or anything suspicious. Remember, this could be a trap, but we need Rueben-Z's blood so I can analyze it for the virus. Any questions?"

Marshall nodded. "What's the plan for after we get this prick's blood and you analyze it?"

"Good question." Buzz licked his lips. "Once I'm able to get a look at the virus in Rueben-Z's blood and have a better idea what we're up against, we're going to lure him here and trap him in a specially designed cell. It'll contain the virus for whenever its trigger is activated, and the virus gets airborne."

Marshall scratched his chin. "Wouldn't it make more sense to lure him here, take the blood sample, then lock him up?"

Buzz looked like he was about to pull his hair out. "I want to know what we're dealing with first so I can make sure his cell will contain the virus. Plus, I want you all out of here for a few hours so I can think. You people are so loud. There's a reason I lived in a mansion by myself."

Carolyn raised her hand. "I don't have an assignment."

"Oh right." Buzz turned to her. "I have a different task for you. Everyone else, get ready to go."

Rueben and Aki quickly packed for the trip into the city. From the clothing Rosa had purchased, Rueben selected a pair of sleek gray track pants and a black sports hoodie. A perfect contrast to Rueben-Z's white one, and the hood would hide his face if they spotted Rueben-Z. Rueben had also found a pair of Versace shades among the new wardrobe.

Aki grinned when he slipped them on. "Sexy. Versace, huh?"

Rueben shrugged.

"Looks good on you. But didn't those go out of style, like, three years ago?"

He scoffed. "You had to ruin it, didn't you?"

She laughed. She was wearing an inconspicuous golden sundress with a cream silk scarf over her hair and chic designer shades. Together, they kinda looked like a celebrity couple trying to go incognito.

Once they were ready, they headed to the living room to find Buzz. Buzz was talking to Carolyn. "If I can get a blood sample from you, then."

"Sure."

Buzz turned and saw Rueben. "I'll need a blood sample from you too."

"Me? What is this, a maternity test? This isn't the Jerry Springer Show."

"No, it's not, although I find the human interaction on that program entertaining. And equally confusing. No, I need a blood sample for science."

Rueben snickered. "With you, everything's for science, isn't it?"

"I am a man of the mind. What can I say?"

Rueben pulled back his hoodie sleeve and joked, "How many pints you need? I don't want to be light-headed during the mission."

"Jeez, we're not doing a plasma donation or anything. A vial from each of you will suffice. One moment. Let me get the sample kits."

He turned to leave, and Aki said, "What about me?"

"What about you?"

"You don't want some of my blood too?"

"Nope. I only need Repeater blood."

Buzz turned and left the room, and Carolyn winked kindly at Aki and Rueben. "You two look so happy together. Kind of reminds me of Marshall and me when we were younger."

Aki smiled.

"Which version of Marshall?" Rueben asked. "Marshall-Z or Marshall-A?" He realized as soon as he'd said it that it was probably an insensitive comment, but he hadn't meant it that way.

"Both," Carolyn said fondly. "Both parts of my life were such happy times for me. Looking back, coming to Earth-A was a blessing—not a curse."

Buzz returned and handed Rueben a syringe. "For the

Rueben-Z sample." Then he drew his samples from both Carolyn and Rueben. As he finished, Martha and Marshall stepped into the room, dressed in street clothes to make their trip to the police precinct.

"All right, people," Marshall declared behind a pair of gleaming aviator shades. "Commence Operation Z, shall we?"

CHAPTER FOURTEEN

Thursday, May 25, 2:34 p.m.

Martha and Marshall made good time into the city, probably because Marshall had allowed Martha to drive. He didn't complain about the rough, bumpy dirt roads heading out of the Catskill Mountains. He held on and let her do her thing.

Now they stood outside the NYPD precinct building.

She hadn't seen this place in days, ever since she'd requested some days off after the world summit situation. After everything that had happened, her boss Ken Kenneth was glad to give it to her.

"You earned it, Dragone. Why don't you take a few days at the spa, get a cucumber wrap or something?"

No matter how many high-profile cases she solved, she would always be a "lady cop."

She bounded up the steps, then noticed Marshall had stopped. "What?"

He shook his head reverently. "It's been a lot of years since I've been in here."

"Well, you were a hero back then. Still are."

He nodded. "Good to be back, especially with Carolyn back and all. Feels good. Feels right."

Martha peered at him. He didn't ever open up like that. It was an odd thing to hear. She didn't want to ruin the moment, so she said nothing and they pressed on through the doors.

"Dragone!"

She heard it as soon as she walked in. Tom. Tom had been the alpha male on the squad for a while, but once she cracked the Pout case and Kenneth promoted her, his star had fallen. Now he groveled for her favor, which after all he'd put her through, she wasn't about to give him.

"Hello, Tom, good to see you. You might remember Marshall Peet, decorated hero?"

Tom nodded in awe. "They were going to make a movie about you. Weren't they?"

"Yeah, well, it shows how desperate Hollywood is for good ideas these days, right?"

Tom laughed a little too loud and slapped Marshall on the back. Marshall laughed with Tom and glanced around the room. "Yep, looks like they kept this place looking about as good as it was when I was here." One of the fluorescent lights flickered, and Marshall grinned. "To the T."

Tom laughed. "Still the same old shithole, huh?"

Marshall rested his hands on his hips. "I always used to tell the junior officers when they'd complain about the place, 'Well, the jail has a better facility. You don't like it, go down there.'"

Tom chuckled. "It's almost true."

Zach the intern appeared then with an eager grin on his face. Martha shook her head. She didn't know how many argyle blazers this kid had. This one was blue and orange, and he wore it with a light-blue dress shirt, khakis, and Converses.

"Hey, guys! I've got that footage pulled up for you. Oh hey, Tom."

Tom frowned and turned to leave. "Hello, Jack."

"It's Zach," Zach mumbled to Tom's departing back.

Marshall winked at him. "Ah, it's part of it. If you haven't pissed off someone yet, you're not playing the game right."

Zach laughed. "I like that. I think I might use that in one of my books."

They walked down the hall, and Marshall made a face. "You write books?"

"Crime novels, mostly."

"That's a pussy profession, son. For computer nerds and virgins. Real men don't write."

"Oh yeah? Tell it to that stunning reporter I took back to my place." Zach winked at Martha and turned back to Marshall. "What about Hemingway? He went to bullfights and drank like a sailor and fished and stuff. He was a real man."

"And his books are boring as shit. The only people that read those books are kids who have it shoved down their throats by high school English programs that haven't updated their reading lists in about fifty years."

Martha and Zach glanced at each other.

"Okay, what about Hunter S. Thompson? He was a real badass—"

"Yeah, hippie porn."

Martha intervened. "You're not going to convince him."

Zach grinned. "I know. I'm messing with him for the hell of it."

Marshall laughed. "I just might like this kid. Pussy-ass writer, but cheeky."

Martha told Zach, "Believe me, that's a higher compliment than he's ever given his son."

She expected Marshall to respond with something like, "I'd give Rueben compliments if he deserved them," but Marshall stood with his lips pursed. If anything, he looked a bit saddened by Martha's remark. Maybe the Peet family was evolving. Maybe after this was all over, they'd be happy again.

Zach led them to a video monitor hooked up to the security footage tape across from the hotel Rueben-Z had paid for with Rueben's credit card. "Okay, so here it is. I haven't had a chance to go through it all to see if there's something of value on it. To be honest, this technology is so outdated. You might say, antiquated."

Marshall popped his knuckles. "Move aside, young'un. Back in my day, they called me Hawkeye, on account of my skill at efficiently reviewing footage."

"So cool," Zach mused. "Hawkeye. I might use that in one of my books."

Marshall took a seat and slid in front of the monitor. "You're welcome."

"Well, I'll be moving along then. I have some copies to make for Kenneth, and I'm picking up lunch for some of the guys." He glanced at his watch. "Oh, and I have to slice the cake for Jerry's retirement party."

"You really do like it here, don't you?" Martha said.

"It's good book research. And yeah. I do. Anyway, tell Buzz and the crew that I said hi."

"Will do."

"Say, you guys aren't working on some new and dangerous case, are you? I mean, after the excitement at the military base and the summit, everyone just sort of disappeared."

Martha sighed. "We're all uh, taking a bit of a breather."

"Well, don't take too long because Pete's still out there. I'm here if you need my help."

Martha nodded. Her mind was on the mission. Hopefully, they were able to glean something useful from the footage so they could call Rueben and Aki, who by this time would already be parked on the curb watching the hotel. If this was a trap, they needed to know ASAP.

"In fact," Zach continued, "I won another uh, hacking competition on the uh, dark net. I got a sweet new deciphering program. It's so good that it's, like, ten years ahead of its time…Martha? Martha, are you even listening?"

Martha grunted. She and the team didn't need some deciphering program. They needed to know where Rueben-Z was. She turned to Zach. "I'm sorry. This is really important."

Zach nodded. "Just tell Buzz, will ya?"

Martha peered at the footage as Marshall fast-forwarded. "Will do, Zach. Thanks. I'll tell Buzz about it."

"I'll let you get back to it then."

Martha nudged Marshall's shoulder. "Find anything yet, Hawkeye?"

Marshall smirked. "Woman, I'm working on it."

The only things to denote the passage of time on the footage were the cars that went by on the street and the pedestrians on the sidewalk. Other than that, it was just the façade of the cheap hotel.

A few moments passed, and an imposing figure wearing a trench coat and a hood stepped out from the hotel and joined the flow of sidewalk foot traffic.

Martha leaned forward over Marshall's shoulder. "Is that him?"

Marshall squinted, his meaty fingers still skillfully manipulating the controls. The footage slowed as the figure glanced both ways and walked purposefully down the street.

They still couldn't tell if it was Rueben-Z or not. The

figure moved out of sight of the camera and Marshall was about to rewind it when two additional figures stepped out from the hotel. They were big and beefy, with thick beards and wearing plaid flannel shirts.

Marshall shook his head. "Shit. They outnumber Rueben and Aki."

"We've got to let them know." As Martha pulled out her phone, suddenly the fire alarm went off, blasting through the precinct floor with ear-splitting noise.

"That can't be a coincidence," Marshall said glumly. "I think we've got company."

Aki and Rueben sat in Buzz's Jeep outside the hotel, observing the traffic and the building's entrance. So far they'd seen nothing out of the ordinary. No sign of Pete.

Rueben glanced down at the syringe Buzz had given him to take a blood sample from Rueben-Z if they located him. He knew Rueben-Z wasn't going to give it to them without a fight. Maybe Marshall had been right about apprehending Rueben-Z now and bringing him back to Buzz's hideout.

Still, they had a plan, and they were going to stick to it.

Back in front of the hotel, they watched a woman struggling with two young children and some luggage hail a cab. One of the kids was throwing a temper tantrum.

To pass the time, Rueben asked, "What do you think their story is?"

"They're not from the city. They're from Jersey. Or in-state, outside the city."

"Okay." They did have a more suburban look than New York City dwellers.

Aki continued her story. "Dad's away on business like he always is. So mom decides to take the kids for a couple of days in the city. Weekdays, because the rates are cheaper. They have a whirlwind visit to the city, but it ends up being more trouble than it was worth. Way more trouble than it was worth. Now, she just wants to go home. She's going to tell her husband to quit his job because she's going mental raising two kids alone."

The cab pulled up to the curb. The mom dropped a bag, and one of the kids smacked the other one. The mom stood in front of the open cab door, shut her eyes, and visibly drew a breath.

Rueben laughed. "I think you might have her spot on."

"Okay, you do it."

"Hmm…I don't know if I can do it any better, but I'll try. She's not the mom. She's a nanny."

"A nanny? I don't know. She looks too old."

"No, no, no. After her divorce, she decided to go to graduate school and try a new career."

"Uh-huh."

"So, she's having an identity crisis which required quitting her high-paying corporate job and taking a less stressful job. She thought, taking care of kids, how hard can it be? As it turns out, it was much harder than she bargained for, and she half-wishes she could leave those kids in the street and make a break for freedom."

He recalled how stressed out he'd been when he'd first learned about his warping powers. Now, he had a team, and things were better. They could handle anything the universe threw at them.

Aki laughed. "Cynical, but I like it."

The woman loaded the kids in the cab, and it drove away.

They scanned the curb again. No sign of Rueben-Z. All was still quiet. Aki pulled up a playlist on her phone and played it softly through the Jeep's sound system.

He laughed as soon as he heard the first few notes. "Je Ne Sais Pas."

She nodded. "This is their first album."

"Prima Donna Complex. It's the best one they did."

"Yeah. They got too cocky with the second and tried too hard to go back to their original sound with the third. Prima Donna, it's just…"

They said in unison, "Perfect."

She skipped through the first couple of tracks, and the next one started with an accordion and a thick bass line.

Rueben's eyes lit up. "*I Love You, I Hate You.* This one was one of my favorites back when…" He didn't finish the thought. He simply watched the sidewalk and let the lyrics fill the Jeep.

Aki finished his thought, "It reminds you of Rachel?"

He nodded slowly. "Yeah, back then. My life's a lot different now."

"Yeah, it's definitely different."

The Jeep was silent for a few minutes.

Then Rueben smiled. "You know, when I first saw you, you were doing a presentation on 'Proper Etiquette While On Assignment.'"

Aki burst into an embarrassed laugh. "Oh, God, that was total garbage. I remember that."

"I wasn't a field agent at the time, but I did 'go on assignment' from time to time when I had to take the tech van out to CIA locations. It took some convincing for Sven to let me attend. It wasn't garbage—I enjoyed it."

"Well…thank you."

"I could tell you were passionate about your job. It kinda

inspired me to be a better agent. And well, you were serious and funny and…well, you. I wondered what it would take to become the kind of guy who got to kiss you. 'Cause I wanted to be him."

She smiled and turned to him. "Well, at that time the bar wasn't set too high. I was with Mike, remember?"

Good ol' Mike Fury.

Suddenly, Aki straightened and peered through the windshield. "Is that…"

He looked in the same direction. "It's Jim. The homeless guy."

Jim's wild red hair stuck out in all directions as he pushed a shopping cart along the sidewalk. He was slowly making his way toward them, oblivious to the stares that passersby gave him as he muttered to himself.

Rueben glanced at the hotel and back at Jim. He reached for the Jeep's door handle. "He knows things. And he knows Carolyn. I think we should go talk to him."

CHAPTER FIFTEEN

Thursday, May 25, 3:01 p.m.

Rueben and Aki exited the vehicle. Aki called out cheerily from ten feet away, "Hey, Jim. How's it going?"

Jim saw them and looked unconcerned by their presence. "The birds live underground and fly like snakes with clocks and dragon wings."

Rueben had no idea what that might mean. "I'm glad you remember us. Would you like to get a bite to eat?"

Jim stared soberly into Rueben's eyes. "The eggs are in the wind, and the books eat the cat. But the horse is in the dell."

"Jim, are you hungry?"

He started to wander off with his shopping cart.

Rueben called after him. "Hey, Jim, wait. Come back. You might be the only one who can really help us."

"Time waits for no man."

Rueben was quick with a response. "But it waits for me."

A slow smile spread across Jim's face, and his lips moved as if he were trying to memorize the quip.

Aki asked him, "Have you seen the other Rueben? The older one?"

Jim ran his finger down the side of his face.

Rueben grinned. "Yeah, the man with the scar. The bad one. Have you seen him? Did he come out of this hotel?"

Jim shrugged and started walking away again.

"Come on, Jim, talk to us. We need your help." Rueben noticed the man's shopping cart was full of old newspapers. "We'll buy you all the newspapers you want. Just talk to us. Help us find the man with the scar."

Jim stopped and looked at his papers. He held up one.

Rueben read the name of the paper at the top in bold letters. "*Paper Warriors*. Hm, never heard of them before."

Jim handed the paper to Aki, and she held it up so that both Rueben and she could read the front page. The headline of one article announced that polar bear populations were soaring. Another claimed that the president had died a year ago, and his clone was now in office. It was an alt-science conspiracy paper.

"Where did you get this?" Rueben asked quickly.

Jim pointed toward a dumpster in an alley a ways back.

"You found it in the trash?"

"The only news there is. And people just throw it away. Knowledge is power. You cannot know what you have."

Rueben had an idea. "Jim, what do they say in those papers?"

"It's the only real news. They are the only ones that know the truth."

"The truth? The truth about what?"

"The worlds. All of them."

Rueben was nodding now. "So this newspaper talks about time warping and world-hopping?"

"She was in it."

"My mother? Carolyn?"

Jim's eyes glazed over as if he was beholding a miracle.

Rueben's mouth dropped, and he met Aki's eyes. "My mom said she did an interview with an alt-science paper that had launched the incident with Thorne. *Paper Warriors* must have been it."

"Might be worth checking out…" Aki flipped the paper over, searching. "Look, here's their address. It's not far."

"I say we go."

"You think we should take Jim out there with us?"

Rueben shrugged. "If he wants to go."

"But what about the plan? Watching the hotel for Rueben-Z? Getting a blood sample for Buzz?"

"To be honest," Rueben said, "this feels like a trap."

"I was getting the same feeling too. What if Rueben-Z has been watching us the entire time?"

Rueben didn't want to think about that. "There might be something up with this paper. Something we can use to understand this time disease situation better."

Aki turned to Jim. "Jim, do you want to go with us to get new papers?" She pointed at the Jeep, and Jim nodded vehemently. He held out his hand, and Aki gave him back the paper. Then he left his shopping cart and marched toward the waiting vehicle.

Jim smelled as if he hadn't taken a shower in weeks and Rueben winced at him sitting on Buzz's leather seats. Then again, Buzz also blew up his own house.

Jim got in the backseat and Rueben settled behind the wheel this time. In the passenger seat, Aki pulled up the Brooklyn address for *Paper Warriors* on her phone GPS. They were only about half an hour from it.

They pulled out onto the road.

Jim lay down in the back seat, seeming to lap up the luxury of the plush leather seating. "So nice."

Rueben kept his eyes on the traffic in the rearview mirror. "I'm glad you like it."

"You know, she didn't know. She didn't know."

"Who didn't know?"

"You mother…she didn't know."

Rueben soothed him. "I know. She thought she was doing the right thing. We've made up. It's all good."

"It's all good," Jim repeated, childlike.

Rueben took a turn, dictated by Aki's phone GPS. "So, Jim. You never answered us earlier. Have you seen the man with the scar?"

"I have not seen him, and the time is short, my friends. It is short for this world."

Rueben gripped the wheel and glanced up in the mirror at Jim in the backseat. "The time disease?"

"The end is near… The end is near, and the creatures turn to dust."

Aki gave Rueben a worried look.

Suddenly Jim pointed at the sky through the window. "For us all. It is time. Like all the other times."

Rueben realized that he was gripping the wheel tight. "You're talking about the time disease the bad Rueben carries?"

"The destroyer of worlds."

Aki jumped into the conversation. "Are you…originally from this world?"

Jim considered this before saying, "No. I like this world best."

"And the bad Rueben destroyed your old world?"

"He destroyed many. They shrivel like dust. He hops like a frog to the next. The cycle repeats."

Then Rueben remembered something Jim had once told him. "We want to end the cycle. You mentioned I had to undergo a quest?"

Jim looked sad. "Quest. Yes. Back to the dead world. Back to the dust world." He cringed and emitted a low groan as if he were physically in pain. "Or else this world dies too. I like this world. You must stop it." Jim started hitting himself. "Stop it. Stop it. Stop it."

Aki reached behind her seat and grabbed his hands. "Hey, hey. There's nothing bad happening right now. Right now we're having a peaceful drive through the city."

Jim drew slow, deep breaths. "The spreading death is peaceful. But it turns everything to dust."

Aki gently released his hands. "We won't let it."

Jim whimpered and was quiet. Aki and Rueben didn't say anything either for the rest of the drive.

The newspaper's headquarters was in a tiny brick building in a seedy part of town. It was next to an overgrown basketball court and a closed-down furniture store.

"You sure this is it?" Rueben asked.

Aki stared at her phone GPS. "This is it. *Paper Warriors.*"

Rueben parked against the curb and squinted across the small strip of grass in front of the building. Iron burglar bars covered the glass door and window. "Let's do this."

Weeds had sprouted through the cracked sidewalk. They brushed against their shoes as the three of them made their way to the door. Jim twiddled his thumbs.

Right before they reached the door, Rueben's phone rang. He answered it. "Hey, Martha. What's up—"

"Rueben?" In the background, sirens wailed, and people shouted.

"Martha, where are you?"

Martha yelled over the commotion, "...police station... attacked..." The rest of her words were unintelligible.

"I can't hear you. What's going on?"

"Rueben-Z...minions survived..."

"Minions?"

Aki yelled, "Rueben!"

Rueben jerked his head around to see one of Rueben-Z's robot minions—burly arms, beard, and lumberjack flannel— trotting up to them over the decrepit basketball court.

It raised one thick hand up and backward with a basketball balanced on its palm. The next thing Rueben knew, the basketball was flying straight at him. He raised his hands but was too late. The ball knocked the air out of him as his back crunched against the brick wall behind him and he crumpled to the ground.

CHAPTER SIXTEEN

<u>Thursday, May 25, 3:12 p.m.</u>

The other lumberjack minion crashed through the precinct building's third floor like a juggernaut, shoving desks aside that were mounted to the floor, sending paperwork into the air. As intimidating as his burly physique was, his verbal silence was even more unnerving.

The building's fire alarm wasn't silent though. It was droning on and on like the trilling of a giant insect.

Martha grabbed Marshall's wrist and tugged him around the corner. Marshall was already panting.

"We can't just run from that asshole. We got to stand and fight."

"With what?" Martha said. "It's an unstoppable robot."

"Honey, nothing's unstoppable." Marshall stopped and picked up a heavy golf outing trophy from an officer's desk. A moment later, the lumberjack robot stepped around the corner, and Marshall chucked the trophy at it. The award clattered off the robot's barrel chest. It stopped.

"Ha! I think I wounded it."

The minion slowly turned and started walking away from them.

"What a coward. I scared it…oh fuck."

The lumberjack robot bent and wrapped its massive hands around the sides of a commercial printer, lifting it with ease. The power cord tore free from the wall as the robot launched the printer Marshall's and Martha's way.

They barely avoided death by printer.

Martha guided Marshall to her boss Kenneth's office. He'd just hung up his phone and was drawing his service pistol. "Dragone? The fuck is going on—"

The office wall caved in as the lumberjack robot shouldered his way in. Sparks shot out from the wall, and the lights all flickered off in the building. The fire alarm, thankfully, also died.

The robot raised both arms with its meaty fingers splayed out like bear claws. Kenneth opened fire, and his bullets ricocheted off the robot's torso and face.

"Come on," Martha shouted as she grabbed Ken's shirt and pulled him toward the office's doorway where Marshall was now standing.

Even though the lights were out, the sunlight coming through the windows lit up the floor. The lumberjack robot crashed through the wall from somewhere behind them.

"Where's everyone at?" Martha demanded.

"The fuck is that thing?" Ken kept saying. "It's not human. It can't—"

Martha slapped the man, and his eyes focused on her. Maybe he'd fire her for that after this was all over, but at least he might survive it if he listened to her.

Marshall stepped in front of Ken. "It ain't human. It's a machine."

"L-like the Terminator?"

"Yup."

"Oh shit—"

"Where the hell is everybody?" Martha asked again.

"Jerry. Jerry's retirement party on the ground floor. They better have saved me some goddamned cake."

Martha took the lead and guided them toward the elevators. "Damn. No, the power's out…" She changed direction and headed for the fire escape.

"Duck!" Marshall called.

Martha ducked as a fire extinguisher shot over her head and crashed into the window. Glass blasted outward and fell in shards to the street below.

"Christ," Ken sputtered as a burst of cool wind swept papers up into the air.

Marshall helped Ken up. "That robot might be dumb as a box of hammers, but he's a strong bastard."

Martha pulled up short when she saw the door to the fire escape. Several tall filing cabinets and a sideways mahogany desk blocked it.

"Not so dumb after all." Ken ran his hand through his sweat-slicked hair.

Martha dialed Buzz's number as she, Marshall, and Kenneth crouched against the cabinets in the breakroom. The robot had trapped the three of them on this floor, and if they didn't do something fast, it was going to find and kill them.

At least the fire alarm was off so she could think more clearly. The smell of burnt coffee annoyed her, though. Someone had left the pot on the burner for too long again.

"What did you do to piss that thing off?" Ken checked how many rounds he still had in his pistol's magazine.

"Its master is a time warper from a parallel universe who we stripped of his time-warping abilities."

"Umm…okay?" Ken massaged his forehead and closed his eyes.

"Come on, Buzz, answer," Martha said.

Marshall leaned against the cabinet with one hand for support. With a grimace, he said, "We need to find a way to show Ol' Metal Head we mean business."

Kenneth looked at him incredulously. "How are we supposed to do that?" He winced at the sound of computer monitors smashing to pieces somewhere outside the breakroom.

"We need firepower."

Kenneth held up his pistol.

"No. Something bigger. Much bigger. You got an evidence room on this floor?"

"Well, yeah."

"Anything that goes bang?" Marshall made an explosion gesture with his hands.

The phone in Martha's hand stopped ringing. "Hello?" a woman's voice answered.

Martha kept her voice to a whisper. "Carolyn?"

"Oh, Martha. How are you…are you near a trash compactor?"

Martha could barely hear her over the sounds of destruction outside the breakroom. "Buzz. Where's Buzz?"

"He's in the lab. I'll go get him…"

"Wait," Martha said but air was already whooshing past the phone in Carolyn's hands. Martha turned to Marshall and Kenneth.

"There's nothing like that in the evidence room," Kenneth said slowly.

"Well goddamnit, it was worth a shot—"

"But there is something in my office. Locked in my desk drawer."

Marshall's eyes told him *Yes, yes, go on.*

"A smoke grenade…"

Marshall waved him on. "And…"

"And what?" Kenneth swallowed. "That's it."

"A goddamned smoke grenade? That's all you got? I thought you were gonna say you had a…something that went boom."

"Ah, Martha," Buzz answered cordially. "To what do I owe the pleasure—"

"What's the quickest way to disable your lumberjack robots?"

"Say what?"

"You heard me. They both survived the mansion blast, and now one is after me and Marshall, and the other is probably after Rueben and Aki."

"Oh dear…"

"Tell me!"

"Water."

"Water?"

"Bob doesn't like water. Now it won't short circuit him completely, but it will slow him down a bit more. Might start suffering some malfunctions."

Heavy footsteps approached the breakroom, and Martha held her breath. All was quiet.

For a moment, it seemed like it would stay that way. Then a swivel chair smashed against the other side of the door. There was another heavy footfall and a fist punched through the door. When the robot withdrew its hand, the door came with it, tearing from its hinges. As it stood there blocking the entry, trying to get the door off its wrist, Martha got to her feet and searched the breakroom for a weapon.

She lunged toward the coffee maker and grabbed the glass carafe. Bob the robot had succeeded in freeing his hand when the carafe exploded on his chest, splashing his chin and neck and upper body in scalding coffee.

"Rrrr-rrr." Bob stumbled back a step from the doorway out into the hall as a few tiny sparks snapped and hissed from beneath his red and black checkered flannel shirt. A moment later the shirt combusted into flames.

Marshall fist-pumped. "All right!" He clambered to his feet and selected a break room chair. Then he hobbled out through the doorway and raised it, bringing it down across the robot's shoulder. The robot swatted it away, knocking Marshall backward to the floor.

"Marshall!" Martha said as she rushed out into the hall and checked on the man.

He groaned. "Will I make it?"

"Just a bump." She helped him up as Bob started to recover. Behind her, Kenneth exited the breakroom. "Go and.. get the smoke grenade."

Kenneth nodded and took off running through the ruined office.

"The window," Marshall muttered as he and Martha picked their way through the ruined floor.

"The window?" She glanced down at the phone in her hand. She must have hung up on Buzz by accident.

"We've got to throw that motherfucker out the window— it's our only chance."

The robot stomped around somewhere behind them, blindly knocking into desks.

"How?"

"We lure it over by the broken exterior window. Then we use the smoke grenade to disorient it. Then I push it out the window."

"Are you crazy?"

"More than a little. That's why I've got to try."

Bob had righted himself then. The fire had gone out on his chest, exposing a set of impeccably defined abs. He tromped toward their position. Martha and Marshall picked their way through the demolished floor until they met up with Kenneth. In one hand, he held the smoke grenade—it looked more like a canister with a pin you pulled—and in the other, an inhaler.

"I've got to sit somewhere." He handed Marshall the smoke grenade. "My lungs…"

Marshall laid a hand on Kenneth's shoulder and nodded.

While Kenneth disappeared to find some cover, Marshall turned back to Martha. "You ready?"

She glanced over her shoulder to make sure the robot wasn't coming yet. "Marshall, don't take this the wrong way, but your hip is busted, you're overweight, and you're older than you used to be."

"Damn right. It's time I got to it."

Martha shook her head. "You're going to get yourself killed. I can't let you do this."

"Yes, you can, and you will. I'm going to give you three good reasons why. One, you need to be backup in case I fail. The others need you more than they need me. I know that. You know that. Two, I am your superior officer, and I am ordering you to help me—"

"Don't pull bullshit rank on me. I'm not going—"

Marshall cut her off. "And three, I have been a useless, mean son of a bitch for a decade now. I aim to change that. I need to do something that matters. I need this. Now, you gonna help or not?"

Martha pursed her lips. "Fine. But we do this together. I'll lure it toward the broken window. I'll drop the smoke grenade and get out of there. And you...shove Bob out the window."

"Aye-aye, kiddo." Marshall gave her a salute.

"Hey, over here!" Martha shouted, and the robot turned its head toward her. She headed for the broken window and fake-slipped on the floor.

"Rrr-rrr." Bob started for her.

Martha clutched her ankle. "Help, my ankle. I think I twisted it." She tried not to sound too fake. Judging by the renewed vigor in Bob's steps, she hadn't overdone it.

Martha regained her footing and fake-hobbled behind a desk close to the window. The wind blowing through it whipped her hair up. Before she left the cover of the desk, she pulled the pin on the smoke grenade and dropped it in a wastebasket. Bob was soon right up next to her, and he took a powerful swing at her.

She ducked his blow, admiring the robot's six-pack as she backstepped. Smoke was now pouring out of the wastebasket and quickly filling the room. "You're up," Martha said as she sprinted away from the broken window.

She stopped and turned back and listened. She didn't hear anything. "Marshall? Marsh—"

"Yippie-ki-yay—" Marshall charged through the smoky

room wielding a wooden coat tree like a lance. Time seemed to move in slow motion. She caught his eyes for a moment. Then he disappeared into the smoke. There was a *crunch* and a *whoosh*, then nothing.

"Marshall?" Martha took some steps closer to the window. Now the wind was blowing smoke in her face as well as whipping her hair. From the street below came a *crash* and several car horns. "Marshall? Marshall? Please tell me you didn't fall out too."

"Who? Me?" Marshall was grinning from ear to ear, lying on the floor beside the window.

Relieved, Martha edged up to the opening and peered out. Bob the robot was lying on the street.

"He dead?" Marshall called, still on the floor.

"He's not moving… Ouch." Martha winced as a garbage truck ran over the robot. "Yeah, he's dead."

"Good. Now can you please help me up? My lower back…"

She helped him up. He wasn't injured—just old. A few minutes later, a SWAT team breached the stairwell door. Medical personnel poured into the room, and Martha indicated where Ken was. Then she and Marshall slipped out of the building.

She would call Zach later to see if she still had a job. But now, they had more important matters to attend to.

CHAPTER SEVENTEEN

Thursday, May 25, 3:12 p.m.

Rueben had enough time to pick himself up off the ground and suck in a painful deep breath before the lumberjack minion was upon him, towering over him like a red and black checkered behemoth. It drew back one massive fist to pulverize him.

"Hey!"

The robot glanced over its shoulder, and Aki delivered a kick to its back. It didn't faze it. The robot turned back and saw that Rueben had gotten away. It searched for him as three gangly men rushed outside the *Paper Warriors* building, one of them with a camera in his hands.

The lumberjack minion turned and studied them curiously.

"Hey," one of the three papermen said, "is that, like, Paul frickin' Bunyan?"

The robot took a lumbering step toward them. One of the papermen started filming. "Sir, what's your name—"

The robot swatted the camera from the man's hand.

"Hey, what the heck, man? That wasn't cheap."

One of the man's companions grabbed him by the shoulder and pulled him back a step. The robot took another step forward, but before it could attack the papermen, Rueben snuck up on him from behind with a tire iron from the Jeep. He swung it at the back of the robot's head, and the iron made a loud *clang*.

The papermen gasped, and the robot turned and tore the tire iron from Rueben's hands. After sending it soaring over the basketball court, it grabbed Rueben by the neck in one meaty hand and suspended him off the ground.

Organic Jim shuddered and stood by the door.

The papermen watched in stunned surprise. "He's not human."

"No. Can't be."

"Then what is he?"

Aki rushed forward and kicked the robot in the groin, but all she did was hurt her foot. The robot raised Rueben even higher off the ground while shoving Aki back a step with his free hand. "He has to have a weakness!" she said as she caught herself before she could fall.

"Are you a superhuman species?" one of the papermen called.

"Are you reptilian? Nephilim? Abominable snowman?"

Rueben's face was beet red. He could barely breathe. He stopped trying to tear the robot's hand from his throat and took a good look at his opponent's face.

The robot's lumberjack face was ruggedly handsome and windblown. While up close, the beard and mustache looked very real, its eyes did not. They looked robotic. Cold.

With his life slipping from him, Rueben jabbed one hand forward, his fingers connecting with the robot's eyes. He felt them swivel under his fingers like marbles, and the robot released its grip on him.

Aki helped him up as soon as he hit the ground.

"We…come in peace?" one of the papermen said.

Rueben was about to tell the three men to get lost before they got themselves killed when his phone rang. Martha. "Yeah," Rueben answered as he dodged the robot's fist.

"We survived. Hope you're okay…"

"Little busy at the moment." He sidestepped a fist that crushed the brick wall behind him into powder. He put the call on speaker.

"What happened to your robot minion?" Aki asked as she stepped up behind the robot and flung a loose chunk of concrete at the robot. It crumbled on the back of the robot's head.

"We killed it."

"Killed it?" Rueben used some of his old ballroom dance moves to quick step to the robot. Using the combat skills he'd learned when training for the Pout mission, he planted a disabling kick to the side of the robot's knee. The knee didn't budge and the robot backhanded Rueben, sending him skidding backward in the grass.

"Threw it out the window. Maybe you can do the same?"

"We're already on the ground." Aki shook her head. She dodged a robot punch. "And the building in front of us is only one story tall."

"What kind of building?" Martha asked.

Rueben glanced up at the robot as he tried to pick himself up from the grass. The robot lunged forward and would have stomped Rueben in the gut had he not rolled to the side at the last moment. "Newspaper place."

"You followed Rueben-Z to a newspaper place?"

"No," Aki said. "We came across Jim outside the hotel. He helped lead us to this place."

"Hullo," Jim said bashfully, waving to the phone in Rueben's hand.

"Maybe there's a weapon of some sort inside the building?" Martha offered.

Rueben rose to his feet and dashed over to Aki. "Let's get inside."

"But we'll be trapped—"

"Water," Martha said. "Throw some water on Bob. That'll slow him down."

"Thanks." Rueben said goodbye and hung up. Then he threw open the door, and he and Aki and Jim dashed inside.

"Bro! Whattaya doing?" One of the papermen threw up his hands.

"Yeah, why you gotta be inviting trouble onto our doorstep?"

Aki scoffed as she turned and slammed the security bolt home on the closed door. "Trouble? You guys excel in trouble."

The third paperman bit his fingernail. "Not when it's trying to kill us, we don't. You guys should leave—"

From outside, the robot Bob barreled into the iron burglar bars fixed to the glass door. Bouncing back a step, he tried to pull the door handle. It sheared right off in his powerful grip.

"I knew those bars were a good investment," said the third paperman.

Bob gripped two of the vertical bars and wrenched the whole door from the frame. He raised it over his head like

Tarzan and the glass inside cracked and sprinkled over his head and shoulders.

"Ah man, no one's gonna believe us without our camera," the second paperman whined.

"No one's gonna believe us if we're dead," the third one said.

Rueben stepped in front of everyone so that he was closest to the robot. "No one's going to die. Now we need a plan." He scanned the building's interior. The robot stood outside the doorway about five yards from him. Beyond the entrance, on the other side of the room were several desks and computers. Each had a bottle or glass next to them.

Behind Rueben was a waist-high wooden counter, and behind it, an extensive array of metal printing presses and relevant supplies. The papermen and Aki were right behind the counter, and Jim had wandered off to inspect the presses, childlike wonder in his eyes.

"If we can slow it down, we might be able to lure it over to the printing press."

The three papermen glared at Rueben as if he was suggesting he torture a baby.

"You can't do that!"

"You have no authority!"

"Free country!"

"You want to die then?" Aki said. When none of them said anything, she pierced Rueben with serious eyes. "I'll start throwing water at it—"

The robot lumbered into the building, one of his massive shoulders knocking out part of what remained of the doorway. It didn't say a word, only trudged toward Rueben and the counter behind him.

Aki wasted no time in hopping up onto the countertop

and scooting over the side. She landed on the balls of her feet, crouch-rolled, and sprang toward the computer desks.

When the robot turned his head her way, Rueben picked up a silver paperweight of an alien head and hurled it at Bob's back.

"Hey! That's a collectible."

Rueben disregarded the comment as he searched for his next projectile to buy Aki time. He hopped over the counter and found an empty plastic water pitcher. He thrust it at one of the papermen. "Fill this up."

"Where?"

"I don't care. The kitchen. The bathroom—"

"You want me to put toilet water in this?"

"We don't have a bathroom," one of them said sadly.

Across the room from them, Aki reached the first computer. She lifted a bottle of green juice, tore off the lid, and chucked it at the robot.

"Hey! My green juice…"

The liquid spattered onto the robot's chest as it started to stomp toward Aki. Tiny sparks hissed, but the lumberjack minion didn't slow.

Rueben found a sharp pair of scissors behind the counter. He launched it like a throwing knife and it embedded in the robot's back.

"My favorite scissors…"

Aki now picked up a glass mason jar half-filled with what looked like a milkshake. She threw it at the robot. The container broke, and milky soup ran down his front. Sparks started to shoot along its leg.

"Rueben, a little help?" Aki said as she reached for the third bottle, a plastic squeeze bottle that looked like it had plain water in it.

Rueben's hands closed around a roll of packing tape and he threw it at the robot.

"Really?" Aki said, right before she released her final projectile.

Rueben shrugged, grinning when the robot's other leg and one arm started to shoot sparks due to Aki's liquid. It was moving slower now with only a desk between it and Aki.

With a jerky but surprisingly fast movement, the robot kicked out, sending the desk against Aki's chest.

"Aki!" Rueben called as she lay on the floor under the broken desk. She didn't move.

The robot turned and faced the counter, sparks dancing along its cheek and jaw as it gave a demented half-sneer. Then it started Rueben's way like a slow, determined bull.

Rueben and the papermen backed away from the counter as the robot tore right through the wood. "Rrrr-rrr." One of its eyes was wiggling loosely in its socket. Aki must have doused its face with that last bottle of water.

"The press prints tomorrow but it also prints today."

"Not now, Jim," Rueben said as he backstepped, trying to figure out how he could use the printing press as a weapon.

"Please don't hurt my baby," one of the papermen whined.

The paperman with the pitcher came out from a side room. The pitcher was half-filled with a yellowish liquid. "Dude, there's no bathroom, but I had to go so I…"

The robot trudged forward and shoved the paperman back against the wall. His pitcher of yellow liquid splashed onto his shirt and floor.

"Dude, did you just piss yourself?"

"No."

"Ah, so unsanitary."

The robot halted, eyeing the liquid on the floor, evaluating how to proceed.

Rueben quickly inspected the metal struts and gears of the printing press. He saw plenty of knobs and time stamps of past and future dates. Suddenly the time stamp clicked and whirred as the date adjusted itself. The press hummed to life and started to print a paper. *Odd...* "How does this thing work?"

"We have no idea," one of the papermen said.

"It just spits out papers with random dates on them. It's like they come from other worlds. Parallel worlds. Crazy shit happens in some of them. The other day we got a paper from twenty years in the future. Front page story said the world was dying."

Rueben's gut clenched. Was this newspaper printing press somehow connected to the multiverse? And could they possibly use this press to communicate with the other worlds?

"Yeah. It's so weird, bro. We copy and print the papers, and people buy them."

The robot was finally starting to edge around the puddle. It must really not like liquid...

"Where's your boss at?" Rueben said.

The man with the pitcher raised his hand from the floor. "That'd be me."

"Just you three work here?"

"Uh, yeah."

"We're screwed, aren't we? Oh no, the alien robot's coming for us!"

Rueben didn't even look the robot's way as he reached up and messed with a plastic cartridge connected to the press. He managed to pry loose a small hose from the cartridge, and sludgy black ink dribbled down the press and his arm like blood.

Ink. That might work. He glanced over his shoulder at the robot, which was lumbering toward him, almost right on him. Now it raised both hands toward Rueben to finish him, its mouth open in a wide grin.

"Eat this."

Rueben wrenched the tube away from the printing press, and ink squirted against the robot's teeth and ran down its throat.

The robot's hands closed around Rueben's shirt collar. Then there was a small explosion, and part of the robot's back peeled back as metal innards sprayed over the floor and wall. With a soft, "Rrrr-rrr," the robot teetered sideways and crashed to the floor like a statue.

"Aki!" Rueben sidestepped the robot's body and slipped through the hole in the counter. He dashed across the room. Aki still wasn't moving, and he couldn't tell if she was breathing.

Grunting, he lifted the desk off her and carefully rolled her onto her back. Her head rolled lifelessly to the side with the motion, and he was preparing himself to give her CPR when her eyes opened groggily.

Rueben had never been happier to see those dark brown eyes of hers than right then. He bent down and kissed her, and she kissed him back.

"The robot?" she said after they both drew a breath.

"Inked."

"Inked? Oh, is that what that black stuff is on your hand?"

Rueben nodded proudly.

"Then why do I smell urine?"

"It's a long story." He helped her up to her feet. Luckily she could stand and hadn't been hurt too bad. Suddenly he had an idea. He pulled out his cell phone and dialed Buzz's number, but it went directly to voicemail. He called again. Voicemail. "That's not good. We better head back to Buzz's."

"Why are we headed back? We haven't gotten Rueben-Z's blood sample yet."

Rueben met her eyes. "Because I think Rueben-Z knows about the Bat Cave. I think he's been watching us or listening to us this whole time, waiting for us all to—shit."

"What?" Aki said.

Rueben recalled what Marshall had told him back at Buzz's mansion. "Split the party."

Yep, they no longer needed to find Rueben-Z. He had already found them. Buzz and Carolyn were all alone and defenseless and definitely not expecting him…

CHAPTER EIGHTEEN

Thursday, May 25, 10:00 a.m.

With everyone except Carolyn finally out of his bunker for the day, Buzz could think for a moment.

It's difficult being me. He poured himself a Scotch from the mini-bar. "Morning be damned," he cursed as he downed it in one gulp.

Buzz knew too much. *Saw* too much.

Where the rest of the world saw an ordinary tree in the park, Buzz noticed the ecosystem within and on the tree and the intricacies of photosynthesis made possible by the sun.

However, life does not stop to allow one to contemplate trees, so by the time he finished taking in a tree, the world was screaming for his attention about things like bike route rules or the flying soccer ball headed straight his way.

Often, the sensory input was too much, so ordinary life exhausted him quicker than normal people. This was why he lived alone and numbed himself with massive amounts of alcohol and sexbots. Life was easier that way.

That, and because he could.

Now that everyone was all gone, Buzz could focus on one thing at a time and get something done in his lab. It wasn't as well-equipped as the one back at his mansion, but it was still top of the line.

He'd already prepared the blood samples from Rueben and Carolyn and was waiting for his computer to spit out its analysis of them.

Back when Rueben had first come to him with his warping powers, Buzz had run every test he could think of so he could study it. Now he felt that Rueben-Z had some kind of virus in his blood that, once triggered, became airborne and ravaged all living organisms as the time disease. It was a long shot, but it was all they had to go on at the moment.

Since Rueben and Carolyn were also warpers, he'd compare their blood samples first until Rueben and Aki returned with Rueben-Z's blood sample. Then hopefully he could figure out how to keep the time disease dormant or figure out how to make a vaccine or cure for it. Then they could worry about finding a way to warp back and undo all the worlds it had destroyed without the disease perpetually coming back.

That was the plan, at least. At the moment it seemed impossibly hard. At least one of the worlds was twenty years ahead. It would take some incredible genius brainpower to solve this problem.

The lab was an all-white room, set up with bright lights and stainless steel surfaces arrayed with touch-screen computer panels, dials, and switches. Suddenly, his printer whirred and started to print out the results of the two blood tests.

The pages contained a bunch of genetic jargon that he understood perfectly well from his time working as a consultant with the CDC. He still had access to its resources and databases and figured he'd probably need them shortly

He prepared a slide of Carolyn's blood and inserted it into his expensive microscope. He'd configured it so he could see the contents on his computer screen. Then he opened the CDC database on a second computer monitor and took a look at the blood sample.

Everything seemed normal—a bunch of red blood cells, as expected.

He then inserted a prepared slide into his electron microscope, and that's when he made his discovery—pulsing spider-like viruses among the red blood cells. Although they had tendrils, they didn't move. They appeared to be dormant, not interacting with the red blood cells, but they were no type of virus that Buzz had ever seen before. He leaned back in his chair.

He thought about what Carolyn had said about a virus or alien invasion killing her world. Was that what he was looking at? The virus that had killed her Earth and all the other Earths? The time virus?

He took another look at it. It sat there, almost as if it was staring back at him. Taunting him. He uploaded its image into the CDC's database to check for any information on it. A warning flashed across the screen, based upon several viruses that most closely resembled its makeup: "Unknown pathogen, likely fatal."

But from what he was seeing, the virus appeared to be dormant in Carolyn's bloodstream. If it was inert in Carolyn's blood, did that mean it was active in Rueben-Z's blood? It was presumably inactive until whatever triggered it to become the airborne pathogen they'd dubbed the time disease. So many questions flooded Buzz's mind. What was the trigger? Did the

Repeating gene neutralize the virus? If another Buzz had determined that Rueben-Z was the destroyer of worlds, why did the virus remain dormant in Carolyn's blood? It made sense that she had it since she traveled with Rueben-Z to all those worlds, but it didn't make sense why it affected her differently. Hadn't Carolyn said that hopping to new worlds reset the time disease? Why?

Buzz hurriedly tested Rueben's blood sample and not surprisingly, found no trace of the time virus in his blood. He needed to do more testing…

A few hours later, frantic footsteps entered the lab and Buzz spun. "Carolyn? Do you think you have it?" His assignment for her had been to go through her memory to see if she could discern when Rueben-Z first started showing signs of the time disease so they could try to pinpoint Ground Zero for the disease. He'd given her a self-hypnosis voice recording to help her with the process.

She shook her head and thrust his smartphone at him. "It's Martha."

Buzz took the phone. She and Marshall were at the precinct, and one of his Bob robots was trying to kill them. He explained to her that Bob's weakness was water.

After he'd hung up, Carolyn looked at him. "How did that robot know where Martha and Marshall were? Do you think it's possible that Rueben-Z knows about this place?"

"Of course it's possible," Buzz said. "But we should be relatively—"

"—safe?" a sneering voice cut in.

Buzz and Carolyn turned to the lab's entrance.

Rueben-Z stood shaking his head at them, wearing a trench coat over his metallic body armor. "Just because I can't warp anymore, you really shouldn't underestimate me."

There was a *swish* of air, and Carolyn glanced down at her chest at the tranquilizer dart protruding from it. Rueben-Z eyed her, his fingers still together in a dart-throwing pose.

Carolyn started to waver then, and Buzz watched, stunned as she buckled and collapsed in a sprawl to the lab floor.

Rueben-Z chuckled. "No warping today, Mom." He turned to Buzz. "Just you and me now, *buddy*."

Buzz felt his face go pale. His mind worked frantically to find a way of surviving this encounter. "Hello, Rueben-Z. I mean, Rueben. Drink?"

"Rueben-Z? That's new."

"We're ahh, calling your home world Earth-Z. That makes you Rueben-Z."

"Interesting. I'm surprised you didn't use Greek letters as on the other worlds when I sought you out."

"Funny you should say that. I was in favor of Greek terminology...but why don't you tell me why you've come here? Seeking my help too? Sure thing. We can try to figure this thing out together."

"Nope. I'm over trying to figure this thing out. I'm ready to die."

Buzz stood there with a stainless steel table between him and Rueben-Z. "You...came here so I could kill you?"

"No. You misunderstand. I came here so I could go out with a bang. If I'm lucky, I might get to take out the whole lot of you One-Deathers before you get me."

"It doesn't have to be this way."

Rueben-Z started to edge his way around the table. Buzz moved in the opposite direction. "No. But I want it to be."

Buzz was sweating profusely. "You know, I don't believe you're redeemable. And probably, neither does your mother."

Rueben-Z growled.

"Sure, she um doesn't want us to kill you, but then again she did abandon you…uh. Shit. But uh…Rueben…he still believes in you."

"Does he now? Hah. Figures."

"We don't want to hurt you. We think you're the key to undoing the time disease." Buzz backstepped slowly away from his aggressor.

"Time disease? That's new too. But I'm not interested in being anyone's lab rat."

"Lab rat?" Buzz uneasily chuckled as he edged in front of a stainless steel lab refrigerator. "No. Nothing like that. We want to work with you. Together. No one has to die horribly."

Rueben-Z snorted. "Ironic, coming from you. Considering how many times you horribly killed me on my world in the name of science."

"One. That wasn't me," Buzz said. "Two, you warped back each time so did I really kill you? Three—"

Rueben-Z took another menacing step forward. "Enough chatting. Let's see if you scream like you did in the other worlds." He shrugged off his trench coat and raised his arm, the metal tube running beneath it gleaming in the lab's fluorescent lighting. Fire didn't shoot out of this tube—frosty ice did.

Buzz ducked while throwing open one of the refrigerator doors. The door frosted over and made *cracking* sounds.

"And the hunter becomes the hunted. I think I'm going to enjoy this," Rueben-Z roared. "Say hello to my little liquid nitrogen blaster." He discharged another icy burst at Buzz, who stumbled to the floor and scrambled under one of the stainless steel tables. Beakers and science equipment froze solid and shattered.

"This isn't you!" Buzz cried out as he dashed through his lab, placing as many obstacles as he could between him and his attacker. "You may be a parallel Rueben, but I know Rueben, and he'd never do this. The virus must be messing with your head—"

"My head is fine." Rueben-Z coated the ceiling above Buzz with ice and Buzz scrambled for his life through the frosty air.

Part of the ceiling caved in behind him, but Buzz kept moving, gasping for breath.

"Death by ice-skating, perhaps?"

Buzz dodged to the side as the floor he'd been standing on skimmed over with ice. On the other side of the patch were the stairs leading up to the living room area. If he could just make it up those steps, he could lock Rueben-Z down here until Rueben, and everyone else arrived.

"Feeling lucky?" Rueben-Z called out. "Go ahead. Try it. I'll give you a head start."

Buzz didn't know if he was honest or not, but he had to get out of here or at least try.

He sprinted toward the ice patch, throwing out his hands to try to steady himself. He started sliding, and at first, he thought he'd be able to keep his balance. Then he lost it and fell and slid into the base of the steps, hurting his ribs.

Rueben-Z laughed harshly behind him as he trudged confidently up to Buzz.

Buzz tried to shoot to his feet, but his feet kept slipping out from under him. Right before Rueben-Z reached him, he was able to throw himself forward, and he started clambering up the steps. He was at the top step when he felt Rueben-Z's hand grip him by the shirt collar, hoist him into the air, and throw him into the living room. Buzz landed on top of a glass coffee table, which shattered. He choked and gasped for breath as he rolled over.

"Nice digs." Rueben-Z proceeded to ice over the living room interior, coating the sofas and tables and walls in ice. "For a polar bear, maybe."

"You're…not funny."

"No, I'm hilarious."

Buzz glanced around the room as Rueben-Z started toward him.

"You can try to call for help, but I disabled all communications before I let myself in."

"How'd you know about this place?"

"I've been to many worlds. I've conversed with many Buzzes."

"Right." Buzz was about to give up hope when his eyes landed on the button concealed beneath the end table a few feet in front of him. Miraculously, it had survived the onslaught of ice. Buzz crawled toward it, each movement hurting his sore ribs.

"Crawling under a table now? Still a coward, I see."

"What…do you mean?" Buzz asked as he inched toward the table.

Rueben-Z stopped walking as he explained, "It may surprise you that I was there at the Canadian border a few months ago, observing as you and your gang attempted to apprehend Pout's microwave bomb. I saw how scared you were when the trucker took you hostage. Hah. Pathetic."

"Oh? Oh yeah? S-so are you. Instead of dealing with life, you decimate it."

"What would you know about decimating life? You haven't seen what I've seen."

Buzz was almost to the table. "Of course I haven't. But admit it, Rueben, you need me. You wouldn't be where you are without me. That's why you find me wherever you are—whatever the world. I'm the only one you can count on. Now you want to kill me for it?"

Rueben-Z snorted and laughed bitterly. "You know less than I thought you did." He lunged at Buzz, but Buzz had already sent his hand up and smacked the button under the table. As Rueben-Z lifted Buzz by the back of his shirt, one of the doors opened, and Biddie sauntered in, wearing denim short-shorts and a midriff tank top.

"Yes, Buzz?" Then she saw Rueben-Z and his intentions for Buzz, and she flexed on the balls of her feet. She raised her hands in front of her. "Intruder, you are like, so overmatched. My programming has jujitsu, karate—"

Rueben-Z raised his free arm and blasted Biddie into a perky block of ice. "She seemed nice," he said flatly and shoved Buzz forward into the air, where his body connected with a frozen couch that shattered under his weight.

"You may be a bit different in each world, but you know what I can't stand about you, Buzz? Your ego. You know what I think? Everything you've ever done for me, I don't think you do it for me. You do it for yourself so you can end up in your precious CR magazine. Here's a little tip—on my world, you do make it. But by then, no one gives a rat's ass because the magazine's dead and washed up. Your issue sells a mere five hundred copies. In both print and digital. Three months later, it goes out of business."

Buzz picked himself up, fighting through the pain in his ribs, and threw himself at Rueben-Z who swatted him to the side. As he fell, Buzz struck his head on the wall or the floor. He couldn't tell.

Through foggy vision, he watched as the front door opened, and Marshall and Martha stepped inside. Martha's eyes widened at the sight of Rueben-Z. "Oh shit."

Rueben-Z stopped and turned toward the visitors. "If it isn't the cavalry."

The room fell silent, and Marshall took long, hard steps, his shoes echoing against the floor. "Now you listen here, son. I don't know who you think you are, but goddamnit, on this world I'm your father, and you'd better goddamn respect that."

Rueben-Z raised an eyebrow. "Nice speech. I'm sure the Rueben on this planet is pussy enough to be intimidated by it. You did a great job with him. Truly. You raised one hell of a sniveling little—"

"Cut the bullshit," Marshall said. "I'm proud of my son. We've come to terms here, on this world. And it was about damn time. Me and him. We're good now. Sorry that it looks like you and your father never got the chance."

The comment hung hard in the air, and for the first time, Rueben-Z looked stung. Then he regained his resolve and glanced from Marshall back to the liquid nitrogen blaster under his arm.

It was at that point that Buzz's vision went black and he passed out.

CHAPTER NINETEEN

Thursday, May 25, 7:13 p.m.

Rueben and Aki arrived back at Buzz's hideout in the Jeep. It had been a long drive, and Aki had driven like a maniac. They pulled into the underground garage and parked next to Martha's and Marshall's Jeep. Rueben exasperatedly clicked off his seatbelt.

Aki shut off the engine. "What?"

"Let's just say that your driving would have scared a mere mortal."

"Well, considering you're not one, what's the problem?" She laughed, and they both got out of the vehicle.

Upon seeing Martha and Marshall's Jeep, they relaxed a bit. They'd been in such a hurry to get back because they hadn't been able to get a hold of Buzz's phone. When he'd called Martha, he'd found out that she and Marshall were going to arrive just before them. She said she'd call him if there was trouble.

She'd never called him back. Maybe Buzz and Carolyn

were busy with the blood samples or whatever they were doing. Regardless, Rueben felt like he could relax now.

He and Aki exited the garage and headed for the front door. Rueben wrapped his arm around Aki. She winced slightly from the pain of the table falling on her back at the *Paper Warriors* office, but she leaned into him and wrapped her arm around his waist. It felt so good to have her next to him. He felt like he could take on the world with her by his side.

They arrived at the front stoop of the hideout, a small sitting area comprised of a wrought iron bistro table that Marshall and Carolyn had claimed as their own. It was empty now, containing only a couple of empty beer bottles.

Nothing seemed out of order.

They opened the front door and descended the trap door. Still good.

Then they stepped into the main level living room and found it all a mess of ice and puddled water. Broken glass lay everywhere, and Biddie stood lifeless.

Rueben *crunched* up to her. Water was dripping from the robot's humanoid skin. Large patches of it remained frozen. "What the hell?"

Aki shook her head. "She's been murdered."

They both looked at each other. They didn't have to say it. *Rueben-Z.*

That's when Emma the kitchen robot entered the room with a piece of paper taped to her metal chest. On it was a note.

Meet me in the greenhouse. Or else.

Rueben and Aki crept down the hallway to the greenhouse. Rueben carried a pool stick in his hands, and he had a billiards ball in his pocket in case he needed it. Aki clutched a paring knife in both hands, liberated from the kitchen. They'd asked Emma for weapons, but she hadn't been able to help them. It seemed that Rueben-Z had reprogrammed her.

"You ready?" Rueben whispered as they edged up to the reinforced greenhouse door, which was slightly ajar.

Aki nodded, and they slipped inside.

They saw no sign of anyone. A canary hopped along the limbs of a tree somewhere above them, chirping out a tune. Beside them, a stream burbled. When they sneaked up behind some tall bushes, they finally saw them.

Their wrists were all bound out in front of them, and they were all gagged. Marshall sat with his back against a tree trunk, and he had a black eye. Beside him sat Martha with a bruise on her cheek. Carolyn was slumped over on the ground sleeping. Out of all of them, Buzz appeared to have taken the worst beating. He had plenty of cuts on his face, and it looked like glass or sharp ice had torn his clothes in places. Judging by the way he scrunched up against a rock, his ribs hurt.

That bastard's going to pay, Rueben thought as he searched the greenhouse for Rueben-Z. At least they were all alive. How had he got the jump on Carolyn, a Repeater? Had he knocked her out with a sleeping serum, like when he'd kidnapped Rueben?

Rueben stole another peek at his friends through the bushes. Martha happened to be looking his way, and she blinked her eyes wide as if there was danger.

"Glad you both found the place," Rueben-Z's voice called

from off to the side. A moment later he emerged from behind some trees.

"What do you want?" Rueben asked.

"I want to challenge you to a little game of hand-to-hand combat. What do you say? Fight me?"

Rueben stared the man down, trying to figure out his angle.

"You win, and you get your friends back. I win, well, you can always warp back and kick my ass."

"Don't do it," Aki said. "Don't play his game. If he knocks you out or puts you to sleep, he can do whatever he wants."

Rueben-Z threw his hands into the air. "I only want an even fight. To see who's a better fighter. You, or me. What do you have to lose?"

Rueben turned his gaze to his friends. Buzz was trying to send him a message with his eyes, but Rueben wasn't understanding. It was probably a warning not to fall for Rueben-Z's trap.

Aki stepped forward and addressed Rueben-Z. "What's to stop me from freeing them right now?"

"Just try it. I've buried explosives in the ground around them. With a press of the remote in my pocket, they go boom. From what I've gathered, you're not supposed to be warping, or it might trigger the virus."

"He could be bluffing," Aki said.

"I'll face you." Rueben prepared to toss his cue stick to the side.

"Oh no. By all means, keep the stick." Rueben-Z sneered. "If you think it will help you."

They stepped up to each other to face off in a grassy clearing. There was a four-foot-deep pool beside them.

"What are the rules?" Rueben asked.

"Fight to the death. Of course."

"So this is about you dying and getting rid of your mess?"

Rueben-Z shrugged. "Or you dying. It'll feel good to get to kick your ass—even if I don't remember when you warp back. Oh well." Suddenly he stepped in and landed a quick jab to Rueben's jaw. Stumbling, Rueben stepped back and brought his guard back up. He swung with the cue stick, and Rueben-Z stripped it from him and tossed it into the pool.

Rueben-Z turned to Aki. "Don't try anything. Remember. Bomb."

Aki looked like she wanted to spit at the man.

Rueben and his opponent circled, taking the occasional jab at each other. They each landed punches, and after a few minutes, Rueben started to tire. He still had his combat training though, and a pool ball in his pocket he could use as a weapon if he got in close. On a thought, he decided to play up his weariness to prompt Rueben-Z to make a move.

At the moment, Rueben-Z wasn't taking the bait. "You're a real bastard, you know, for taking away my warping ability."

"Maybe you not being able to warp is the only thing stopping the time disease from destroying this world."

Rueben-Z shook his head. "Nah. I don't think so. This world is as doomed as the rest of the worlds I've been to. It'll die. And there will be nothing you can do to stop it."

Rueben raised his dukes, feigning fatigue. "We'll figure out a way. I have a team, remember? You're all alone, and it's killing you."

That made Rueben-Z grimace. He unsheathed a combat knife from under his shirt. "Well, at least I won't have to bear it for much longer." He lunged at Rueben, who barely dodged the strike.

"We can still work together. We don't have to try to kill each other."

Rueben-Z swiped again, nicking Rueben's arm. "This only ends one way. Come on, give me your best."

Rueben grunted as he analyzed Rueben-Z's motions. Rueben-Z had the greater combat expertise, and he was bigger. What Rueben needed was the help of his friends, but Rueben-Z had the bomb.

Rueben knew then that he had to get the remote. Then Aki could help their friends.

Rueben-Z lunged again with the knife. Rueben countered Rueben-Z's arms with his wrists. Then he charged in close as one hand grappled with the knife hand and the other darted into Rueben-Z's pocket. It was empty.

"There's no bomb!" he shouted to Aki.

Aki sprinted across the grass to where everyone sat or lay in the grass. She started cutting through Buzz's bindings first.

Rueben-Z roared as he elbowed Rueben in the face and shoved him to the grass. "I'll kill them all!" He made to rush toward Aki and his hostages, and Rueben caught Rueben-Z by the ankle. With a grunt, Rueben-Z fell to his chest, and Rueben leapt on top of him.

Rueben-Z kicked him off, and Rueben started punching him repeatedly in the face. His knuckles had blood on them from Rueben-Z's nose, and he kept on punching until Rueben-Z finally blocked him and got in an uppercut to Rueben's chin.

"Go ahead. Get mad. Feels good, doesn't it?"

Rueben wiped his face on his sleeve and attempted to throw another punch. Rueben-Z caught it. "You've still got much to learn." He shoved Rueben hard to the ground, but as Rueben fell, he slung the pool ball up at Rueben-Z. It connected with his temple, and he crashed down beside Rueben with a *thud*. Dizzily, Rueben-Z raised his blade and was about to bury it in Rueben's heart when his eyes went wide and the knife slipped from his grasp. Then he slumped over unconscious.

Buzz crouched behind Rueben-Z with a syringe in his hand.

Rueben drew a deep breath as he recovered. "Nice jab."

"Why, thank you. That felt good."

"What was in the needle?"

"Knockout serum. From that asshole's body armor."

Rueben eyed his opponent's body armor. It contained many hidden compartments and secrets, he was sure. "What gave you that idea?"

Buzz shrugged. "He used it to knock out Carolyn down in the lab. It was either that or throw him into that pool and carbonite freeze him like Han Solo."

"Huh? Are you joking?" Rueben peered into the pool beside them in the grass.

"No."

Over by the trees, Aki was finishing up freeing everyone's bindings. Rueben joked, "I don't believe you."

Buzz shook his head. "There's no guarantee he'd have survived though, without his warping ability. At least now we can interrogate him."

Everyone else was walking over to them now. "How would you have frozen him?"

"Science." Buzz grinned. "Tell you what, once we save the world, I'll carbonize you just to prove I can do it."

Rueben smirked. "You're offering to kill me as a reward for saving the world?"

"For science. Now I have a completely self-contained and

sealed cell for this jerkoff. I've got some sore ribs. Maybe you and Marshall could do the heavy lifting?"

CHAPTER TWENTY

<u>Friday, May 26, 7:01 a.m.</u>

Buzz paced the living room in his silk robe and slippers. His chest was all bandaged up, and he was irritable as he waited for Emma to bring him a beer and aspirin.

Emma brought them to him and began cleaning up the mess in the living room. Everyone else sat on the few remaining pieces of furniture that had survived Rueben-Z's icy wrath the night before. They all wore bandages and winced when they moved what hurt them.

"Well, people," Buzz said. "We have Rueben-Z in a sealed-off cell in case he somehow triggers the time disease. Don't want this world destroyed by it. We still have to figure out what to do to reverse the damage on all those other worlds."

"Have you tested his blood yet?" Rueben asked.

"It's processing. I'm also inspecting his high-tech body armor. Thank you for removing it from him, Marshall."

Marshall sat proudly, his arms folded over his chest.

"Now, if we are to get to the bottom of this time virus, we're going to have to determine Ground Zero, which has to be on Earth-Z. Carolyn. You were writing down all the memories you had on Earth-Z of Rueben-Z right up until he started showing signs of infection…"

"Signs of infection?" Martha said.

Carolyn stood. "Rueben-Z wasn't always like how he is now. He used to be less aggressive, less prone to immediate anger. If you study his face close enough, you might see involuntary eye twitches and tremors. I believe it's his way of fighting the virus in him. I just don't know if it's too late for him."

"I don't think it's too late," Rueben said. "We can figure this out."

Buzz nodded. "In that case, I'm going to head back to the lab. Carolyn, maybe you could fix us some of those chocolate chip cookies I've heard so much about? After what we've all been through, we could use a treat."

Buzz paced his lab, wired on coffee.

Notes and printouts littered his workspace, and he had scribbled all over the floor and tables with dry erase markers —the lab tables were handier than paper.

Now, he knelt on the floor and began to scribble, trying to understand what he'd read in Rueben-Z's blood tests.

A quick rap on the door interrupted his thoughts, and Rueben walked in with a plate. "Thought you'd want some breakfast, John Nash."

Buzz didn't look up from his crouch upon the floor. "What have I said about making fun of *A Beautiful Mind*? Just leave it on the counter." Rueben set the plate down, and Buzz winced at where he'd set it. "No, not there. You'll mess up the calculations."

Rueben lifted the plate. "Okay."

Buzz stood, exasperated. "Here, I'll take it." He took the plate, and the sight of eggs and toast did remind him that he was indeed quite hungry. He plopped onto a stool and dug into the meal. There were a couple of Carolyn's cookies, too, but he set them aside for the moment.

Rueben sat across from him on another stool. He gestured toward the notes all over the room. "I'm having flashbacks to our Columbia days. What is all this?"

Buzz smiled around his mouthful of eggs. His mathematical calculations had been the dominant decoration in their dorm room. They suited him much better than Rueben's poster of some moody emo French band. "I'm trying to understand the composition in Rueben-Z's blood. It's not normal."

"Of course he's not normal. He's a Repeater."

"I know that, but…the time virus has completely infected all the cells in his body. Yet, they still appear to be dormant, all performing their normal functions as if unaware of the virus there."

Buzz paused to finish his meal. He dusted the crumbs off his hands. "This virus. It scares me. I can see why none of the other Buzzes could figure it out."

Rueben clapped a hand on his best friend's shoulder. "They weren't you. You can do this."

"Maybe. But this is what's stumping me." He pointed at a calculation that took up most of the floor between them. "It's like this. If X is the pathogen and Y is an unknown time variable, then with the simple manipulation of the Y variable, as you see here, well, you can follow the result to its logical end."

He pointed to the end of the equation about ten feet away. "And that's what happens." Buzz held out his palms and let Rueben grasp the crystal-clear concept laid out perfectly in numbers and variables on the floor.

Rueben frowned. "Okay, Buzz, I don't follow. What does this mean?"

Buzz scratched his head. It was all so clearly laid out on the floor. He didn't know how to explain it any better without the numbers.

"Give me a real-world application."

"A real-world application? Basically, Rueben-Z and Carolyn are carriers of the virus. Somehow, it only becomes active in Rueben-Z. Either she's got some immunity or Rueben-Z was exposed to something that infected him first—made him patient zero. All I know for certain is that once the virus gets 'switched on,' the virus becomes airborne, and it goes all Michael Stipe."

"Michael Stipe?"

"Yeah, Michael Stipe. You know, R.E.M...*It's the End of the World As We Know It?*" Buzz sang the hook in a flat monotone.

Rueben facepalmed. "So you're saying maybe he was exposed to something that Carolyn wasn't?"

"Yes. That's my best guess. His exposure must have been to the virus's original form. I think—and this is only a hypothesis—that since it's a time virus, it mutates each time Rueben-Z warps. Don't ask me how—I don't know. But it would explain the slight differences in the dormant virus in Rueben-Z and Carolyn."

Rueben scratched his head. "I thought you said they were the same virus except the one in Rueben-Z had infected all his cells."

"Try to keep up, man. Or...shit. Maybe I forgot to tell you.

It's the same virus in him but slightly more evolved. I don't want to bore you with how I know, but we were right about you and Carolyn not warping anymore until we knew how it would affect the virus.

"My thinking, hopping to parallel Earths resets Rueben-Z's virus to dormant but warping back in time causes Rueben-Z's virus to go active. Or maybe simply with the passage of enough time, the virus becomes active in him with or without any warps. From what I've heard of Rueben-Z's story, I don't think he's warped much on this Earth if any." He waved dismissively. "I need to do more tests."

"What kind of tests?" Rueben asked.

"If I could safely trigger the virus to activate and mutate, I'd be able to study it further so that I could work on pinpointing its evolutionary track and de-evolving it."

"I don't know. Sounds like a big risk. We can't chance turning Rueben-Z into a superweapon down here."

"Not Rueben-Z. Only a sample of his blood. If we could figure out what switches it on, we could isolate the variable and ultimately stop the process."

Rueben scratched the back of his head. "Okay."

"If what Carolyn has said is true, the trigger is time."

Rueben raised an eyebrow. "How do we test time without warping? Please don't tell me we have to wait down here for a year…"

Buzz reached for one of the cookies he'd placed aside and bit into it. His eyes lit up. "Your mom's cookies are amazing! No, no. I figured it out. We don't have to warp. We only have to simulate a warp."

Rueben rubbed his chin. "How? Wait, I'm confused."

Buzz was happy to explain. "Rueben-Z carries the virus inside him, and when he hops to another world, this resets the virus back to its dormant stage in him. After his first death and subsequent warp, the virus begins its course. After a few warps, it's a matter of time before it mutates into an airborne form and wipes out the entire world."

Rueben sat up straighter on his stool. "From what I can guess, he hasn't died too many times on this Earth."

"That's good. That's good. That's the only thing keeping it from going apeshit in his blood for this long."

"Are you sure about this theory?"

"Only mathematically," Buzz said. "Like I said, we need to test it."

Buzz fastened on his goggles while everyone else in the lab gathered around what looked like a miniature rocket ship, something a cross between a jet fighter's cockpit and something out of Superman.

"I present to you my prototype for the Buzz Lugger space and time capsule."

"Wow," Rueben said. "How do you happen to have it here in this hideout?"

Buzz beamed. "There's a reason I selected this hideout for us to come to. As soon as Carolyn mentioned coming to Earth-A in a space and time capsule, it reminded me of the one I had started working on in my free time."

Carolyn grinned. "It looks like the one Buzz-Z made on Earth-Z."

Marshall rubbed at his jaw. "Holy shit. You mean that thing can go back in time?"

"Sadly, no," Buzz said. "Not yet. Although the shell is

complete, I don't even know where to begin to manipulate time and space for real. I'm not a Repeater, you know."

"I don't get it then," Martha said. "Why are you so excited?"

"Because while it may not be able to warp back and forth in time yet or hop sideways to parallel Earths, it can *simulate* warping back and forth in time. That's all we need for this test. To simulate the effects of warping on a sample of the virus."

Aki folded her arms over her chest and nodded. "Impressive. If it works."

"Oh, it'll work."

Buzz peered down at his space and time capsule lovingly. While there were three seats for people to sit inside it, there was also a transparent box at the front nestled among the controls. Carefully, Buzz opened it and placed a vial of sealed blood in it. Then he closed the box and operated some controls on the console. He turned back to everyone.

"Now, is everyone up to speed on Rueben-Z and the virus?"

Everyone nodded—Rueben had explained it to them in terms they could understand—but Buzz still threw out a summary. "Both Rueben-Z's and Carolyn's blood contain the time virus. Carolyn's looks permanently dormant while Rueben-Z's...looks like it could come alive at any time. Ironically, the accelerated passage of time is what I theorize awakens it."

Everyone murmured, and Buzz nodded and tightened his goggles. "This device inside the capsule simulates the time travel experience."

Marshall screwed up his eyes. "You're sending the virus back in time?"

"Actually, I'm sending it forward."

"Forward?" Martha said.

"Yes. And don't ask me to explain how…you wouldn't understand. Step back, folks."

Everyone backed away from the machine, and Buzz activated it.

"How far are you sending it?" Rueben asked.

"We're going to start by sending it two days forward."

The space and time capsule sprang to life with roaring motors and whirring fans. It began to vibrate furiously as the contents inside the transparent box experienced the simulation of the passage of two days.

Buzz announced over the roar of the machine, "This should only take a few minutes. But, let me show you this." He wished he would have shown them the control before he sent it, but he had been so anxious to get it going that he didn't stop to explain his thought process. He clicked on a screen and showed them a video. "This is an electron microscope image of Rueben-Z's blood before we sent it."

He pointed at the screen. "This is it. The virus."

"Jesus, it's everywhere," Marshall said.

Aki frowned while Martha raised a hand over her mouth.

"It's fine. It's fine, people." Buzz straightened his shirt. "While Rueben-Z's blood is completely infected, the virus is surprisingly inactive."

"What if it turns active now?" Martha said.

"It's confined to the vial. It can't escape."

Aki eyed Buzz. "This won't somehow affect Rueben-Z?"

Buzz dismissed the notion. "It shouldn't. He's in a self-contained, sealed cell on the other side of the compound."

The space and time capsule *beeped*. The motor cut off, and Buzz opened the transparent box. He donned a pair of rubber gloves and extracted the vial.

"Now, we're going to look at what would happen in two days."

A device connected to his computer had a vertical slot in it. Buzz inserted the vial of blood inside and typed some commands on the computer.

Then he cued up the display screen for the rest of them to see. "This is what happens to the virus after two days."

The time virus-infected cells twitched and swayed, but the motion was so minute as to be unnoticeable.

Rueben commented, "So this means that even though Rueben-Z can't warp anymore, the passage of time still slowly awakens the dormant virus in his blood?"

Buzz studied the computer screen. "A good deduction. Let's try three more days."

Buzz placed the vial back into the capsule. He set it for three more days. While they waited, Buzz set the display screen up so that on the left side was a snapshot before he'd put the specimen back in for three days.

The specimen returned, and in the same manner, Buzz prepared it and brought it up on the right side of the display screen.

There was a collective, "Whoa."

This time the tendrils protruding from all the infected cells were clearly twitching erratically.

"I'm no biologist, but it still doesn't look active," Aki said. "It's just sitting in the cells. Waiting."

Rueben rubbed the back of his head. "I don't like this."

Marshall agreed. "Kinda like we're playing God or something."

Buzz shook his head dismissively. "It's contained. No virus can penetrate a glass vial."

Rueben sighed. He wasn't going to win this argument.

"Now," Buzz said. "Let's see what happens if we pick a longer point. Say, three weeks."

He returned the vial to the space and time capsule.

After a few minutes, Buzz again removed the vial and prepared it.

When the image came up on the display, Rueben's mouth dropped. "Whoa."

Aki rubbed her arms as if she was cold. "Oh my God."

Marshall, Carolyn, and Martha stared at the screen. The virus was now wide awake. As they watched, the infected red blood cells bumped and crashed against each other, their tentacles writhing menacingly. It was so vivid and clear on the screen that it was disturbing to watch.

Aki shuddered. "Can we turn it off?"

Buzz flipped off the monitor, and the group all stood in silence.

Rueben said, "This is bad."

Buzz shook his head. "This is good. We know that we now have over three weeks to figure out how to neutralize the virus in Rueben-Z's blood before it goes full-blown active. It's still contained. It can't escape the vial."

"Then how about we toss this infected blood in an incinerator?" Martha asked.

Marshall nodded in agreement. "I don't much like dealing with viruses and shit."

"We could," Buzz said. "It would be more helpful if we could study this virus in action."

"In action?" Rueben asked. "Are you crazy? You want to release this into the world—"

"No, buddy. A controlled experiment. Down here in a sealed-off portion of the greenhouse."

"I don't like it," Aki said.

Rueben, Martha, and Marshall agreed.

"But I need to study it further so that I can contain and neutralize it."

Carolyn hung her head and turned to the group. "I'm afraid I have to side with Buzz. I know firsthand the effects of this virus in the wild. If Buzz says he can test it in a controlled environment, it might be our best shot at figuring out how to stop it and reverse the damage done to all the other worlds."

Marshall was unconvinced. "It's crazy. I think we're over our heads on this one—"

Carolyn grabbed Marshall's hands in hers. "There are worlds out there that this virus destroyed. As Repeaters, it's our duty to find a way to reverse all that, to restore the worlds if we can."

Marshall closed his eyes and put a hand to his head. He sighed deeply, then stared longingly into Carolyn's eyes. "Aw hell. I...suppose you're right. That's a hell of a lot of responsibility."

Rueben nudged his father's shoulder. "Comes with having great power, right?"

With a smirk, Marshall said, "I taught you well, son." He turned back to Buzz. "So how are you planning to go about this?"

CHAPTER TWENTY-ONE

Friday, May 26, 11:24 a.m.

Buzz stood outside the steel-reinforced door to the greenhouse. He was covered head to foot in a hazmat suit and carried a locked transparent case that contained the vial of Rueben-Z's time disease-infected blood.

Aki looked doubtful. "I just want to be on the record that I disagree with killing the greenhouse."

"Not the whole greenhouse," Buzz said, "only a controlled sample section." He opened the reinforced door via the keypad on the wall and entered the greenhouse, heading toward a part in the back that no one else had seen yet.

A knee-high mechanical-looking robot with treads under it for mobility followed Buzz inside while everyone else stayed back in the hallway. The reinforced door sealed shut behind Buzz, and everyone else watched him via the camera integrated into the robot's "eye." They all watched on a tablet that Rueben was holding as Buzz reached a glassed-in section of the greenhouse with a hermetically sealed door.

Buzz opened it and set the box containing the vial upon

the grassy ground inside. There were a few trees and bushes inside the glass structure. The robot rolled inside too, then Buzz exited and sealed the door behind it.

Rueben and everyone else watched through the robot's eye as they waited for Buzz to rejoin them. On Rueben's tablet, the robot didn't move. A few minutes later, Buzz said, "Hey guys," as he walked down the hallway.

"Where'd you go?" Martha asked.

"Decontamination chamber in the back of the greenhouse."

Aki scoffed. "A decontamination chamber? What don't you have down here?"

"A bowling alley. I don't have a bowling alley." With a grin, he took the tablet from Rueben and started tapping out commands.

The robot's two claws appeared on the screen as it moved up to the box. Then it opened the transparent box and withdrew the vial. Then it uncorked it.

"So that virus," Marshall said. "It's active and ready to kill everything in its path?"

Buzz nodded. "Should be capable of airborne transmission once it infects its first host, according to my calculations."

Rueben scratched his chin. "Host as in grass or tree?"

Buzz nodded.

"Aren't plant cells different from animal cells? How can this virus…"

"It's unlike anything I've ever seen. I don't know how, but it can."

"Think a lab created it?" Marshall asked.

Buzz shrugged. He peered at the tablet, but nothing was happening to the vegetation around the box and the robot in the glass enclosure. Outside the glass enclosure, a canary hopped up to the glass and pecked at it curiously. It flew away. "Hmm. I expected the virus to be more aggressive than this. Maybe it's still not ready to spread to other hosts."

"Buzz," Martha said. "You have a canary in the greenhouse?"

"What better way to tell us if the place has been breached by a stage four deadly pathogen? Not that that will happen."

Martha looked at him, unsure if he was joking or not. "Um, can't you use computer sensors?"

"Are you sure this is safe?" Aki asked.

Buzz looked irritated. "Look, people. Have you ever heard of the Symmalus virus?" They all shook their heads. "That's right. I was a consultant to a joint-CDC task force that found a way to render that particular virus harmless to humans. I've got this situation under control."

They all exchanged glances.

"Plus, I came through with the defense of the summit attack with the Binnies, didn't I?"

They couldn't argue with that.

They waited about a half-hour, but nothing happened. Then they left and went to the living room where they tensely waited a few hours and ate a quick lunch. Still, nothing happened. Buzz left and checked on Rueben-Z to make sure he was still unconscious and sleeping in his sealed cell. He came back, confirming that this was still the case.

"Well," Marshall said with a glance at the tablet screen, "doesn't look like anything is happening. I don't know about everyone else, but after dealing with Rueben-Z and now this virus, I could use some rest and relaxation."

Buzz raised his hand. "R&R? Nah, how about something better?"

"Should we even ask?" Martha said.

Buzz smirked. "I may not have a bowling alley, but I do have a disco bar…"

Martha raised an eyebrow. "There's no oxytocin in here, is there?"

Buzz paused as he flipped on the lights. The room was wide and circular, and colored lasers shot across the floor while mirrored balls danced above them. "Nope. Not unless you want some."

Martha glared at him.

"Right then," Buzz said. "Any questions?"

Marshall offered his hand to Carolyn. "Dance with me?"

She grinned and took his hand, and he swirled her into the room.

Martha whistled. "Okay, one, I thought he wanted to relax. And two, your dad's got some moves."

Rueben just stood there. He'd never seen Marshall move like that. He recalled all the times his dad had given him shit for taking up ballroom dancing. Guess dancing was in the Peet genes.

Buzz flipped on *Stayin' Alive* on the jukebox, and Rueben shook his head. He told Aki, "Isn't this the theme of this month?"

She laughed and pulled him out onto the dance floor. Amidst the colored lights and the music, some of the anxiety and stress from the last week faded away. Here, they could forget the time virus experiment in the greenhouse, even if it was only for a short time. For all they knew, the time virus sample in the greenhouse would never spread on this Earth. There were too many variables they didn't know.

While they danced, Rueben lost himself in Aki's infectious smile, her vibrant energy, and the way her dark eyes twinkled with delight. He wished he had gotten to know her in a simpler time, back when both of them thought that there was only one Earth, before all the craziness with Rueben-Z and the destruction of worlds.

Then it occurred to him that after everything she knew about him, she was still here. He twirled her around and brought her in close to him. "Why are you still here with me?"

"What do you mean?"

"After everything you know about me. Who I really am, where I've come from. Why are you still with me?"

She gazed into his eyes and pushed back a lock of his hair. "Because I love you."

His heart nearly burst out of his chest. "You do?"

She smiled. "Of course. Can't you tell?"

"Why? After everything…"

"Because you're you. You're dorky. I like that. And funny. And capable. Also, you're a good friend to those around you. Shouldn't that be enough?"

Donna Summer now played in the background, and he held her close. The reflection from the mirrored balls washed over them in reds, greens, and blues, and from somewhere, a fog machine pumped piña colada-scented smoke onto the floor.

Rueben basked in the warmth of her body against his and the soft touch of her fingers in his hand. He had never been so happy in his life. He whispered into her hair. "I love you, too."

She whispered back, "I know."

He laughed, and they held each other and danced in contented silence.

Off to the side, Buzz tried to dance with Martha. But he

kept falling all over himself, and they both dissolved into laughter and headed for the bar.

Marshall and Carolyn whizzed by. All they were missing were bell bottoms. Marshall twirled Carolyn, and he chuckled at Rueben. "Son, take a few more dance lessons, and you might someday be as good as your old man."

At this, Rueben and Aki laughed hard.

Marshall raised an eyebrow. "Hey, don't laugh too hard at that—"

Suddenly, an alarm shrieked through the disco room. Everyone stopped, and Buzz flipped off the music. He retrieved a tablet from the bar. "Oh shit. It's the greenhouse. The virus…"

Everyone gathered around the screen. Marshall said, "The virus what?"

Buzz turned and faced them all. "The virus. It got out of the enclosure."

CHAPTER TWENTY-TWO

Friday, May 26, 4:35 p.m.

"Follow me," Buzz said seriously.

"How did this happen?" Martha demanded as they moved down the halls.

"I don't know. Either the glass enclosure wasn't perfectly sealed, or that virus is more permeable than I thought.

"It wasn't that damn canary pecking the glass, was it?" Marshall grumbled.

"No. Now enough talk." Buzz led them to his lab and passed through a door off to the side. They were now in a computer room. It wasn't as big as the one in the mansion, but there were workstations and shelves of servers set up throughout. There was also an impressive wall of monitors at one side that he'd positioned to form one giant monitor.

Buzz quickly queued up a real-time overhead view of the greenhouse from security cameras hidden in the treetops and ceiling. On the giant screen was the transparent enclosure where he'd left the vial and the robot. The inside of the chamber was all dead grass and withered trees, and outside of the section, grass and other vegetation were dying in a slowly expanding circle.

It was horrifying to watch the efficiency by which the time disease traveled, withering all in its path.

"Son," Marshall said, "is this the part where you say we're doomed?"

Buzz shook his head. His face was resolute, like a general's. "No, this is the part where I tell you all to pick a workstation and sit."

"Huh?" Martha said.

Buzz instructed them all to sit in front of the various computers positioned throughout quickly. He selected one himself and typed up some commands. A video feed displayed on each of their computers with the word "Live" at the top corner. There was a thin black crosshair and reticle on each screen like a first-person shooter video game.

"This is Plan B, people. Rule number one of experimental science shit: never don't have a backup plan."

On the big screen at the front of the room, the time disease slowly spread but it looked like it might have been picking up speed.

"What you are each now looking at is the view from a combat bot equipped with flamethrowers, and liquid nitrogen blasters like Rueben-Z had. Hopefully, one of the two methods will neutralize the virus. The controls should be self-explanatory. Just use the joysticks to move your robot and press the two buttons on the top of the joystick to launch the fire and ice. Understand?"

They all nodded grimly.

"Good. Now get to work people."

They each piloted their robot up to the expanding circle in the greenhouse and started to unleash their two weapons.

Occasionally they glanced up at the wall of screens at the big picture to help them navigate and coordinate the attack.

The greenhouse was big and fortunately, the time disease continued to spread outward in a predictable manner.

Buzz winced as he saw a canary fall out of the trees in the infected zone on his computer screen and wither to dust right in front of him. He wiped sweat out of his eyes and sprayed the approaching withering vegetation with liquid nitrogen.

He held his breath and moved his robot backward and watched. It appeared to have worked, and he was about to announce this to everyone else when the withering began anew and started expanding again toward his robot.

"Use the fire, people," Buzz said calmly. "Ice doesn't work."

He glanced up at the big screen to ensure that everyone was tackling the problem properly. Then he switched computer screens and brought up a blueprint of the sprawling underground compound. With all the smoke in the greenhouse, he knew he had to open up the vents leading to above ground. This would be fine, as long as the fire completely killed the virus—it wouldn't be able to escape into the outside world.

It was their only choice. If he didn't open up the greenhouse, the entire compound was in danger from the fire they were unleashing. He opened the vents, and the fire raged inside the greenhouse until the flames wiped out all living organisms. The robots' cameras blacked out one by one as they melted and eventually, the overhead view on the big screen blacked out as well.

"Well, did we do it?" Marshall finally asked.

Buzz breathed a deep sigh. "I think so. I think so."

Utterly exhausted, they all rested afterward in the living room. They all eventually dozed to sleep, except for Buzz, who returned to his lab.

Sometime later, Rueben awoke to Buzz cheering in front of his tablet.

Buzz explained, "I've been inspecting Rueben-Z's body armor. I found a time disease atmosphere detector." He held up what looked like a miniature Geiger counter.

Everyone started waking up all around the room. Rueben rubbed the sleep from his eyes. "I thought Rueben-Z and Carolyn didn't know about the disease. They thought it was a curse or alien attack or something."

"While they weren't sure what was causing it, it looks like they did have a way of detecting it in the air. Look, it's tech from twenty years in the future. The good thing is that I've tested the entire compound. The virus isn't down here."

Rueben nodded. "That's good, right?"

"Yes. Extreme heat kills the virus. That explains why Rueben-Z wanted to incite a global nuclear war—to kill potential hosts for the virus to infect—although the plan wouldn't have worked in the end."

Rueben frowned. "That's good that the virus isn't down here with us. But is there a chance that it got out? Above ground?"

Buzz shifted on his feet. "I've pulled up satellite imagery of the area around the base. I don't see any wanton devastation... so I think we're good. This virus is deadlier than anything we've ever seen on this planet in all of human history. Worse than Ebola, worse than the Black Plague—no one's ever seen anything this bad. If it did get out..."

Buzz shook his head with the idea.

Martha sighed. "It sounds like we got lucky."

Marshall bobbed his head. "Damn lucky."

"Good job, everyone," Carolyn said. "But we can't just sit on this. Now that you've all seen what this virus can do, you understand that we must find a way to stop it."

Buzz took a breath. "While I'd like to say that it's as easy as burning Rueben-Z alive…" When no one laughed, he cleared his throat. "That wouldn't fix the issue on all the other worlds it has destroyed. We have to find this virus's origin on Earth-Z. And it's still dormant in Carolyn's blood. We need a cure for it—not just a way to destroy it once it's active in the environment."

Aki eventually asked the question that was on all their minds. "How do we determine Ground Zero on Earth-Z? I mean, not only would we need to know the physical location, we'd also need to know the exact point in time."

They all contemplated in silence for a few minutes. Then Rueben had an idea, but he didn't like it. "There is one person who can help us determine the virus's origin." They all looked at him, and he said it, "Rueben-Z."

Martha frowned. "Buzz said he'll be sleeping for days. He's in a coma."

Buzz sighed. "I can bring him out of the sleep coma."

Rueben saw the unease on everyone's faces. Understandable considering he'd held them all captive down here like a madman. "I think it's our best bet."

Buzz stroked his chin. "I'll prepare the subject."

CHAPTER TWENTY-THREE

Friday, May 26, 6:07 p.m.

They all stood in the hallway outside Rueben-Z's sealed cell. Via the keyboard outside the viewing window into the cell, Buzz commanded the IV line to switch over to a compound that would wake Rueben-Z up.

Rueben eyed the restraints on Rueben-Z's wrists and ankles. There was even a thick steel band around the man's waist. Lying there in a hospital gown without his body armor on, the man looked less imposing than ever before, although his scarred face and chiseled muscles still gave him the look of a hardened prison inmate. Beside him, Rueben saw that Aki was studying the restraints too. She looked like she approved of their effectiveness.

Marshall frowned. "How long until this fancy drug shit wakes him up?"

"Should be an hour, plus or minus five minutes," Buzz said.

"Okay." Marshall stood solemnly at the viewing window with his hands clasped in front of him. "I'll stay and keep watch. Let you all know when he wakes up."

Buzz shook his head irritably. "There's no need. My computer will alert me when his vitals—" He stopped when he caught Martha's cue that he was saying something socially improper. "Right. Be my guest. Stay and watch." He turned to go.

Carolyn stepped up to the window and touched Marshall's arm. "I'll stay too."

The soft smile on Marshall's lips was barely perceptible. "I'd like that."

Rueben rolled his eyes at his parents and turned to Aki. "Tell me we'll never be that annoying."

She chuckled. "Oh, we'll be worse."

Martha snorted. "Be? What about now?"

Rueben and Aki laughed softly, and everyone except for Marshall and Carolyn headed down the hall toward the living room to wait.

Once there, Rueben, Buzz, Aki, and Martha sat in the living room and started playing Uno to pass the hour.

Rueben smirked. "I can't believe we're playing Uno. I haven't played this since I was, like, eight."

Buzz frowned. "I didn't furnish this space expecting company. It's all I've got, and it's the only card game my robots will play with me."

Aki leaned against Rueben. "Well, I think it's a fun way to pass an hour."

Rueben laughed. "Pass an hour. We're waiting for a comatose terrorist to wake up so that we can interrogate him about the deadly virus about to kill the world."

"And it makes you sound all the more adventurous." She pecked him on the cheek, and Martha and Buzz rolled their eyes at each other.

Martha turned to Buzz. "I think you and I should make out, just to get on their nerves."

Buzz's entire body froze, his cards in his hand, and he looked as catatonic as Rueben-Z. "Excuse me, please." He got up and left the room.

Rueben told Martha, "You have no idea what you just did to that poor guy."

"I meant it as a joke."

Suddenly their phones all buzzed with texts.

Rueben read it aloud. "It's Marshall. Rueben-Z's awake."

They all crowded around the viewing window, looking into Rueben-Z's cell. The man still lay confined to the hospital bed, his eyes wandering over the room's interior.

"Can he see us?" Rueben asked.

Buzz shook his head and raised his tablet for Rueben to see. On it was a red circle. "Not unless I press this button. It'll make the window two-way instead of one-way like it is right now."

Inside the room, Rueben-Z began to work his jaw. He licked his lips. "What the hell did you do to me?"

The tablet Buzz held had a microphone icon on it with a diagonal slash currently across it. Buzz tapped the icon, and the slash disappeared as the tablet's microphone unmuted. "We injected you with the same knockout serum you put in Rueben when you kidnapped him before the summit attack. And then in Carolyn down in my lab."

Rueben-Z growled as he narrowed his eyes at the intercom in the room. "Why?" His voice came through the tablet's speakers.

Buzz went on. "Why? You should be grateful we didn't kill or torture you or something. You tried to kill us, you asshole—"

Rueben-Z growled even more furiously. Aki placed a hand on Buzz's arm. "Let me do the talking?"

Buzz handed Aki the tablet.

"Rueben, can you hear me?" she asked calmly.

"What? Not calling me Rueben-Z anymore? This some sort of CIA negotiation tactic to get on my good side?"

Everyone stood tensely, watching Aki. Aki pressed the red circle button on the tablet, and the viewing window's transparency shifted subtly. Aki waited until Rueben-Z realized that he could see outside his cell before she smiled confidently and said, "Yes, we are trying to get on your good side. We're not here to play games. We're not here to keep you restrained, not if you help us."

Rueben-Z's eyes were flushed and reddish. "What if I don't want to help you?"

"A valid question," Aki said. "But both you and us, we're trying to achieve the same goal. We're trying to figure out how to defeat the phenomenon that keeps destroying the worlds that you and Carolyn hop to. We've confirmed that high heat kills it, but we still have to find a way to reverse all the death and destruction on each world, including the world you're originally from."

Rueben-Z thought this over. Then he started wriggling against his wrist and ankle restraints. "Then why are you keeping me locked up like some damn circus animal or lab rat?"

Aki paused. After a glance at Buzz, she said, "We did a little experiment. One involving an infected blood sample of yours."

Rueben-Z gave a smug smirk. "Well, that was a stupid idea. If I'm infected, at least."

"You are, asshole," Buzz said, leaning in over the tablet.

Aki flashed him a stern look, and he raised his hands and stepped back. "The experiment did turn out rather dangerously."

"Shit." The concern in Rueben-Z's eyes was unmistakable. It was there for just a moment. Then it was gone. "It didn't get outside this place, did it? Did it?"

Dropping her gaze for a second, Aki glanced back up to return his stare through the window. "We're not sure. There's a chance it escaped through the air vents, but we didn't have a choice."

A vein bulged in Rueben-Z's neck. "If it got out, this world is fucked. Are you going to let me out now?"

Aki turned to Buzz.

"Yes," Buzz said. "But not until we can confirm that the virus in your blood is still dormant. It's possible that the blood sample we uh, experimented with was somehow able to communicate with the virus in your blood. We haven't had a chance to check your blood again since that. Do we have your permission to take another sample?"

Rueben-Z grumbled something.

Aki said, "The sooner we can clear you, the sooner we can let you out of there."

Buzz reached over and hit the mute button on the tablet. "Are you out of your gourd? That man is not stepping foot out of that cell. We can interrogate him from here."

"We've got to show him we're true to our word," Aki said. "I've overseen plenty of terrorist detainments. As long as you can verify the virus in his blood is still dormant, you can leave the rest to me."

"And us," Marshall said with a nod at Martha. "He's not so scary when he's stripped of all his fancy gadgets and that body armor of his."

Seeing his protest was shot down, now Buzz grumbled. "Fine. I'll get suited up."

A few minutes later, he was inside the cell wearing a hazmat suit and drawing a vial of Rueben-Z's blood. He stepped in an adjoining decontamination chamber immediately afterward.

They all watched Rueben-Z's cell on the tablet screen from the confines of Buzz's lab. Buzz, meanwhile, was finishing up with the blood analysis.

"I just don't understand why he's acting like that," Rueben said. "He's an alternate parallel version of myself, and I'd never act that way. We're trying to help him."

"He's trying…"

Everyone turned Carolyn's way. She spoke louder now. "I've spent the most time with him. And I am his mother. You all probably didn't notice, but he's trying to be good. But…the virus is interfering with his nervous system. I'm almost certain of it."

"Explain," Buzz said.

"When you look at him, you all probably see a crazed dangerous man strapped to a hospital bed. That's only natural. That is who he is to you. But if you watch closely, there are subtle movements to his body that I believe signifies that he is fighting the virus."

She picked up Buzz's tablet and zoomed in on Rueben-Z's face. "See his eyes? The twitching. And the veins in his neck.

His body or his mind is trying to fight this disease. He doesn't want to kill anyone. The virus is driving him mad.

"That, coupled with his conscience…he's inadvertently responsible for the destruction of entire world populations. Sure, he might have been able to deal with that starting out when he believed he could reverse it all. But now he's given up hope. I think…part of him just wants to die."

Buzz grimaced. "Well, we can't oblige him."

Rueben shook his head. "He could have the answer to Ground Zero for the virus. Besides, think of what this could mean for science if you can figure out how to defeat a time disease. They'd put you up on a pedestal beside Einstein. Higher maybe."

Buzz thought about that.

"I know how you like a challenge. You may be the smartest man in the world."

"In the whole multiverse," Buzz posited. "Fine. Fine I'll get behind the idea that Rueben-Z isn't a totally irredeemable shitbag." Suddenly his computer beeped, and Buzz studied the screen. Then he soberly turned to everyone else. "Well, people, the results are in regarding Rueben-Z's blood test to see if the virus is active in him now. Drumroll, please."

No one said or made any drumming sounds.

"You guys are no fun," Buzz whined.

"Well?" Martha said.

"The virus is active."

Alarm spread through everyone.

Buzz slapped his forehead. "The greenhouse experiment— the virus in the blood sample must have communicated with the rest of Rueben-Z's blood in his body, triggered it…"

"What now?" Carolyn asked.

Buzz paused, trying to think. "It's probable that the virus is now airborne inside Rueben-Z's cell. But it's okay. It's completely sealed off and self-contained."

"You said that about the glass enclosure in the greenhouse too," Marshall said.

"The cell is better. I over-designed it, and it should contain the virus. At least, for a while... Look, I just thought of something. I think there may be a way to stabilize the virus in him and revert it to a dormant state."

"How?" Rueben asked.

Buzz patted Rueben-Z's body armor lying on the table beside him. He pressed a button on it, and a hologram of data appeared in the air above it.

Aki peered at it. "It's in code."

"Exactly," Buzz said. "It's from Buzz-Z. It's an instruction manual on his completed space and time capsule."

Rueben inspected the coded hologram. "How can you tell?"

"Because the table of contents is in a code I developed in high school. I think Buzz-Z intended for Rueben-Z to show this to the other Buzzes in the multiverse so they could finish their prototypes of the space and time capsule if needed."

Martha studied Buzz. "If he made the table of contents readable to you, why not put the whole instruction manual in the same code? Why pick something you can't read?"

Buzz looked a little perturbed. "Isn't it obvious? Because this is a friggin' space and time capsule. Can you imagine what would happen if the instruction manual fell into the wrong hands? Nations would kill to have it. Global panic could ensue if the public even knew such technology was possible."

Everyone exchanged serious glances.

"So once you figure out how to complete your prototype

space and time capsule, you'll be able to make the virus in Rueben-Z dormant again?" Rueben asked.

"Yes. By simulating a parallel world hop. It also reasons that resetting the virus from an active state to a dormant will ease Rueben-Z's psychotic tendencies if the virus is messing with his head. Come on, people. Let's review what we know about the virus.

"When Rueben-Z warps back in time, or when enough forward time has progressed, it triggers the virus into an active state. Luckily, since we took away his warping ability, we don't have to worry about that part of the equation.'

Rueben nodded. "I think we're on the same page now. How long is it going to take you to crack the code and complete the space and time capsule?"

Buzz sighed and clasped his hands together behind his back like a lecturer. "It's not the capsule that's the problem. Judging by the diagrams I've been able to view from this holo-gram manual, the shell is complete. I've got all of the rare earth minerals and electromagnets properly positioned. All that's missing is the software that enables the capsule to hop sideways to other worlds as well as warp forward and back-ward. Right now I can only 'simulate' the passage of going forward in time."

"Are we talking hours or days?" Marshall said impatiently.

Buzz dropped his head.

"Months?"

"No. Years."

CHAPTER TWENTY-FOUR

Friday, May 26, 7:40 p.m.

"Years?" It was Rueben-Z speaking through the tablet's speakers. In a display of full transparency, they'd left the tablet's microphone unmuted so that Rueben-Z could hear their progress.

"Um," Aki said calmingly. "It's not going to take that long. We're going to figure this out." She hit the tablet's mute icon. "You can figure this thing out, right, Buzz?"

"Yeah. In about twenty years. This encryption is so complex."

Aki's face sagged, and she turned back to glance at the tablet's screen at Rueben-Z lying on the hospital bed inside the sealed-off cell.

"Wait," Martha said. "I've got it."

"Oh?" Buzz eyed her caustically. "You think you're smarter than me?"

"If we're talking street smarter? Uh, yeah. But no, this has nothing to do with who's smarter than who."

Buzz shoved his hands into his pockets. "Then what are we talking about?"

"Zach."

"Zach?" Buzz said. "He's definitely not smarter than me. Although he's quite good at hacking…"

"Exactly." Martha grinned. "When Marshall and I stopped by the precinct, Zach mentioned that if he could help in any way to let him know. He said he won some black market hacking program that's like ten years' advanced for its time. How about you message him about it?"

Buzz's mind processed this for a few seconds. Then, "I'll get right on it. Once he grants me access to it, I'll be able to feed it a digitized version of the hologram instruction manual. Then I'll know if it can help us or not. It's possible I could have the space and Time capsule up and running relatively soon."

"All right!" Carolyn whooped, and everyone else started to smile.

Except for Buzz. "People. People. Let's not celebrate until I can verify it'll work."

"Cheer up, bud," Rueben said and smacked his best friend on the shoulder. "Like Aki said, we'll figure this thing out. Together. Just let us know what you need us to do."

Everyone essentially stayed out of Buzz's way while he worked. They helped with preparing food for their next meal and continued to monitor live satellite imagery outside of the compound to make sure the time disease hadn't spread.

When the food was ready, they ate, but no one was really

focused on it. Their thoughts were on Zach's hacking program now working on Buzz-Z's encryption.

When Buzz finally exploded into the room with an excited face, everyone felt relieved.

"It worked! It worked! I know how to complete the space and time capsule software!"

They went down to Rueben-Z's cell and spoke to him via the tablet outside the viewing window. Rueben-Z began to sob when they told him Buzz would be able to complete the capsule much quicker than he'd previously thought. Maybe only a couple of days, maybe sooner. Then they'd be able to reset the virus in his blood, and he'd be able to leave the cell and be free again.

Rueben-Z finally spoke in a hoarse whisper, "It's different here." His voice now had a different quality to it, stripped of its bellow and hateful snarl. He sounded like... He sounded like Rueben.

He looked around at them all, and he looked truly broken. "This Earth is different than the others. You all are different."

The comment seemed genuine and started to ease everyone's tension.

"What you're doing on this Earth," he went on. "Buzz, you've never gotten this far. Each time we made progress, something bad happened. The virus mutated again or whatever we're calling what it does." He gestured toward the window at them. "And after all the bad things I've done and tried to do to you all. You gave me a chance. I know you think I'm the villain...but it's this virus. I think it's messing with my head. Trying to control me. Turn me into a monster."

Buzz rubbed his face and spoke to the calmer Rueben-Z. "We won't let you turn into a monster. We are going to help you."

Rueben-Z raised an eyebrow, smiled, and shook his head. "You know, every Buzz has said that and failed at it."

Buzz cleared his throat. "Well, they're not me."

Rueben-Z nodded in agreement, then glanced at Aki. His voice was almost a whisper. "I know you probably hate me. I don't blame you. But you're my… You're my wife…on my Earth. You know?"

He looked at her pleadingly through the viewing window. "I know it's another world. But, back there, you're my home, my other half. And I know you can't see this right now, but in that world, you and I are happy. We're madly in love, and I… I…play guitar for you."

She made a face. "Guitar?"

He gave a slight smile. "I'm not very good, but I'm learning. I write you love songs. And we have kids. Two. Emma and Monty. I chose Emma, and you chose Montauk after that movie *Eternal Sunshine of the Spotless Mind*. You know, with Jim Carey?"

Aki's voice was flat, her eyes suddenly watery. "I know the movie."

"Yeah. He tells her, 'meet me in Montauk.'" Rueben-Z sucked in a breath. "And there's this breakfast cafe next door. On Sunday mornings we sleep in and we order crepes and we watch movies all morning, and the way you look at me is not the way you're looking at me now."

He buried his face in his hands. Rueben-Z was about to come undone.

Rueben put his arm around Aki's shoulder, and she fell into him and gripped him tight.

Rueben-Z saw them and choked back a lump in his throat, a sense of longing washing over his face. "I'm just so glad not to be alone anymore. I'm just…so glad."

After a quick dinner, they were in the lab again as Buzz worked on the software for the space and time capsule. Most of the work he was able to automate to his computer and AI, but now and then he had to step in. With the decoded instruction manual from Buzz-Z, it was almost too easy.

Everyone gave Buzz some distance but were on hand in case he needed something. The tablet was lying on a table. On it, the security footage showed Rueben-Z eating the breakfast Emma had brought him. They'd undone his restraints, and he now sat huddled in a corner eating.

Aki was the first to comment. "Poor thing. It's hard to watch."

Martha leaned back against the table. "I disagree. I know he can help us, but solitary confinement serves him right for all he put us through. How many times has he tried to kill all of us in the past week? He's a psychopath."

Aki took Rueben's hand under the table. "I've dealt with psychopaths and terrorists. This isn't that."

"Isn't it?" Martha said. "Even if he wasn't thinking straight, he still tried to start a global nuclear war. There have to be consequences for that."

Marshall chimed in. "Give him a break. We've got no idea the kind of pressure this guy's under."

Rueben whipped around to his dad. "Are you turning into a softie now?"

Marshall toyed with the table and mumbled, "It's…just… It's kinda hard…your kid—parallel kid—whatever… I was a cop long enough to know that people make mistakes. Good people. Some of them, after they serve their time, they find a way to make amends."

Carolyn patted Marshall's shoulder. "He's right. If Buzz can revert the active virus in Rueben-Z's blood back to dormant, it would truly give Rueben-Z the second chance he needs to make things right once and for all. He could be the only hope this planet has."

Aki nodded in agreement. "Rueben's been right all along. He and Carolyn. They believed in Rueben-Z when all we could see was the bad. I say we inspire him to be the person we know he can be. There's a hero inside of him. He's just lost it somehow."

"Well said," Rueben said with a sly grin. "For a badass special agent."

Aki punched him lightly on the arm. "As much as I love kicking bad guys' asses, I guess I'm a big softie at heart."

"And I love you for it." Rueben planted a quick kiss on top of her head.

Buzz looked like he was about to vomit. "Since when did this story change from a sci-fi action thriller into a Hallmark Channel movie?"

They all laughed, and Martha winked at Aki, giving the special agent her sign of approval in dating Rueben.

Rueben didn't see it because he was facing Buzz. "Back to the point of Rueben-Z helping us once he's clear to leave his cell. How are we going to be able to reverse all the destroyed worlds? How are we going to find Ground Zero for the virus on Earth-Z?"

Carolyn raised her hand. "We could hypnotize Rueben-Z and relive some of his memories from before the time disease destroyed Earth-Z the first time."

"It's a possibility," Buzz said. "But it would be cumbersome and who knows if it would work on a Repeater who did so much warping. I say we go to Earth-Z in the space and time capsule with the virus detector." He raised the miniature Geiger counter-like device he'd found earlier in Rueben-Z's body armor.

"That does sound like it's probably going to be the best option," Aki said.

A thought popped into Rueben's mind. "What if there was a better way to go through Rueben-Z's memories?"

Buzz made a waving gesture for him to go on.

Rueben smiled. "Do you think twenty years ago that Buzz-Z would have given Rueben-Z the same kind of nanobot you gave me when I was first learning about my warping powers?"

On Earth-A, Rueben's nanobot had given Buzz tons of data on his powers when they were trying to figure out a way to stop Pout.

"I reckon he might have." Buzz turned to Carolyn for confirmation.

Carolyn pursed her lips as she thought about it. "Yes. Yes, he did."

Buzz clapped his hands. "Woohoo! That's our ticket. We only need to access the data on his nanobot, and we should be able to watch Rueben-Z's memories through his eyes. Ground Zero, here we come."

CHAPTER TWENTY-FIVE

They were all seated around the conference room with a projector sitting at the front of the room. They'd darkened the lights, and Buzz sat behind a laptop connected wirelessly to the projector. "Let's begin, shall we?"

Everyone sipped their waters and nodded.

"Buzz-Z must have made some adjustments to the nanobot he injected into Rueben-Z. The interface is a little different than mine. Bear with me…"

Buzz brought up several thumbnail video files on the screen and clicked on them one by one, scanning through Rueben-Z's memories on Earth-Z. As Buzz skipped through the more mundane moments in Rueben-Z's life, Rueben was surprised to see Carolyn in a good number of them. She and Rueben-Z seemed really close.

They watched Rueben-Z's thirtieth birthday. It was at a cheesy medieval-themed restaurant called Brave Knight Burgers. Aki-Z sat beside Rueben-Z, smiling as she moved in for a kiss. Buzz skipped forward.

In the next memory, Aki-Z was greeting Rueben-Z as he came home from work. She handed him a small wrapped box.

"What is this?"

"It's for you. Open it."

"Okay. What are we celebrating?"

"Just open it!"

He opened the gift and pulled out an elegant silver watch. "Honey, this is gorgeous, but—"

"Read the engraving underneath."

Rueben-Z flipped the watch around. "Happy...Father's Day? Wha—"

Her face broke into a full grin, and tears sprang to her eyes.

While everyone in the darkened conference room watched the couple embrace, Rueben grabbed Aki's hand and squeezed it. Tears leaked down her face, and he wrapped his arm around her.

The memories played on.

There were drinks with Buzz-Z and more than a few arguments. Friendly arguments though, mostly jostling and kidding around, same as on Earth-A.

They all joked about how weird Buzz-Z's face looked. Carolyn hadn't been kidding about the Botox not being a good idea.

They watched more of the nanobot footage. There were discussions and plans. Experiments in Buzz-Z's lab. Family dinners with the kids.

Buzz fast-forwarded and eventually came to a scene where it was only Carolyn and Rueben-Z and withered grass all around them. Dust or ashes blew in the wind.

Rueben glanced over at Carolyn and saw how hard this was on her. "We're too far, Buzz. Go back farther this time."

Buzz rewound Rueben-Z's nanobot footage until they came to an interesting scene. Rueben-Z was sitting at a conference table glossing over a report that Buzz-Z had slid to him. Aki-Z was also seated at the table.

"What kind of mission is it this time?" Rueben-Z asked.

Buzz-Z explained something about an unmanned tanker in the Atlantic Ocean cruising at full steam toward the coast of NYC.

"What's this about?" Rueben asked, and Buzz paused the nanobot footage.

Carolyn answered. "On Earth-Z, Rueben-Z, Buzz-Z, and Aki-Z were part of a non-government-sanctioned task force that protected the world from global threats."

"Very interesting," Buzz said.

Rueben and Aki exchanged glances.

"What," Buzz said, "was this tanker mission all about?"

Carolyn shook her head. "I don't know. I wasn't a part of the task force, but they often talked about their missions when they came over for dinner. I don't remember any tanker missions though. And I don't recall any missions that involved viruses or diseases."

"This could be our big break," Aki said.

"I wouldn't get our hopes up," Buzz said. He skipped the footage forward past Rueben-Z sneaking past some armed commandos and Rueben-Z was shutting off a valve that was spraying steam into a room. Next, Rueben-Z picked a lock and entered a control room where he communicated with Buzz-Z and Aki-Z. Then he found a metal box with *Nunez* engraved on it.

Rueben-Z started to open the box, and the nanobot footage blanked out.

"Wait, what just happened?" Martha said.

Buzz rewound the footage, but again the nanobot footage blanked out.

Marshall shook his head. "What if that's it? Ground zero?"

Buzz skipped through the nanobot footage and found several more places where it blanked out. "Well, it might be. But there are other places like that too. It could be Rueben-Z's nanobot going out. They don't last forever, you know. We should probably ask Rueben-Z if he remembers what was on the tanker to check our bases."

They brought Rueben-Z up on the tablet and inquired about the tanker incident, but he didn't recall anything out of the ordinary about that mission. He certainly didn't remember finding a metal box. He did remember planting charges on the ship and scuttling it before it reached the NYC shore to cause whatever damage its senders intended to cause. It was a typical mission.

Although this seemed odd, they filed the incident away in their memories when Buzz received a notification that the space and time capsule software was nearly complete. It required some finishing touches that only Buzz could perform.

Perhaps the next morning, they'd be able to use the space and time capsule to reset the virus in Rueben-Z's blood.

CHAPTER TWENTY-SIX

Saturday, May 27, 9:00 a.m.

"Can you believe it?" Rueben said.

Aki looked at him. "What do you mean?"

"What Rueben-Z said about you and me being married on Earth-Z."

They were sitting in the conference room waiting for Buzz to arrive.

"Sure, I can believe it. I saw it in Rueben-Z's nanobot footage." She narrowed her eyes at him. "What's this really about? You and me?"

Rueben scratched behind his head. "Yeah. I guess. I mean, it almost seems meant to be. Doesn't that...I don't know. Make you feel weird? Like you've already seen a taste of the future?"

She smacked his arm. "Regardless, I still want to be with you. After hanging around you and your friends for so long, not much weirds me out anymore." She smirked. "Rueben Peet, you're not getting rid of me that easily."

He chuckled. "Fine by me."

Buzz strode into the conference room then. In his hands was a thin rectangular plastic container. He set it on the table up front and popped open the lid.

"People. People. In a few minutes, we are going to try to reset the time virus in Rueben-Z's blood by putting him in the space and time capsule and simulating a parallel world hop. I've just finished my last-minute checks on the capsule's software, and it should work."

Whoops and cheers went up from around the room.

"What's in the box?" Marshall asked.

Buzz grinned and lifted a syringe from the plastic box. "Needless to say, I've been busy. Didn't get much sleep last night because I was working on protection."

Martha frowned. "Protection?"

"Yes. From the time virus."

"So, a vaccine?" Aki said.

"Not exactly." Buzz sighed. "I'm not sure how to explain it to you all except that this injection should protect us from exposure to the time virus. It's active in Rueben-Z, after all, and I always have a backup plan.

"Basically, once injected, we shouldn't be able to contract the virus so that means all us normal people should be immune to turning into a withered pile of dust in case something goes horribly awry. Rueben, you should be fine, and Carolyn's virus appears to be permanently dormant, but you'll both get the shot as well. Any questions?"

"Yeah," Marshall said. "You may be a genius, but since when do you have the knowledge or means to build impromptu vaccine things?"

"Point taken. Remember how I mentioned being on a CDC task force to eradicate another virus? This is one of the techniques we developed from that project. It still has an experimental treatment classification, but it was easy enough for me to replicate it down in my lab here. I still have access to the CDC databases, and I had Rosa procure and deliver the necessary equipment during the night. Satisfied?"

Marshall shrugged. "I say, let's get this all over with." He pulled back his shirtsleeve. Everyone else did likewise, and Buzz proceeded to give everyone their shots.

Afterward, Buzz announced for everyone to follow him to Rueben-Z's cell.

As they walked, Martha rubbed her injection site and asked Buzz if there were any known side effects.

"It is possible you may spontaneously grow a second pinky on your left hand."

"Are you joking?"

"Yes."

"Not cool," Aki said, but Rueben couldn't help but chuckle.

They arrived outside Rueben-Z's viewing window and peered inside. Rueben-Z looked like he was meditating, which added another layer to his tough-guy persona. The space and time capsule sat outside the back of the cell by the decontamination airlock that led into the room.

It took all of their combined strength to move it into the airlock. Then Buzz instructed everyone to step back and he closed the airlock behind him and opened the passage into Rueben-Z's cell.

Everyone watched from outside the cell's viewing window as Buzz pulled out the virus detector device. The readings were off the charts, but Buzz wasn't wearing a hazmat suit, and he wasn't starting to wither. Then Buzz opened the capsule and instructed Rueben-Z to sit in one of the three seats. Buzz strapped Rueben-Z in and manipulated the controls to simulate a world hop. Buzz closed the capsule and stepped back. The device began to vibrate.

Martha was studying the capsule intently through the window. "So that thing is really going to travel back to Earth-Z?"

"That's what Buzz says," Aki said.

"There are only three seats," Martha said. "Who's going to be going?"

When no one said anything, they all turned to face Rueben. He shuffled his feet. "Buzz was going to make the announcement later today. After the virus in Rueben-Z is reset back to dormant."

"And…" Martha prodded.

Rueben sighed. "It's going to be me, Buzz, and Rueben-Z."

Marshall nodded grimly. Carolyn didn't say anything. Aki looked concerned, but she didn't say anything either.

Inside the cell, the space and time capsule stopped vibrating.

Buzz opened the capsule and helped Rueben-Z climb out. Then Buzz drew a deep breath and checked the virus detector. He turned the device toward the window so that everyone else could see it.

There was now no virus inside the cell.

CHAPTER TWENTY-SEVEN

Saturday, May 27, 1:46 p.m.

They were back in the conference room, all of them, including Rueben-Z. He'd had a chance to shower and was now dressed in one of Buzz's silk robes. Rosa was out buying him some clothes, but she wasn't back yet. Instead of sitting at the tables like the rest of the group, Rueben-Z stood off to the side, leaning against the wall like Hugh Hefner with a scar on one half of his face.

Rueben glanced over at Rueben-Z, wondering what the man was thinking. The V of his robe revealed the top of two chiseled pecs that Rueben wondered if he would ever develop on this Earth. The man's arm muscles were also to be envied, folded across his chest as he silently absorbed Buzz's recap of everything they knew.

The man, once their arch enemy, now exuded a sense of tough, regal pride that said he wasn't a man to be messed with, especially not his family and friends. Of course, they weren't all one big happy family. Rueben caught Marshall and Martha staring distrustfully at Rueben-Z at intervals.

"So that's it," Buzz finished.

Everyone in the room looked confused.

Martha groaned. "How about we get the Cliffs Notes version of the plan? Minus all the science jargon."

Now Buzz groaned. "Very well. To sum up our plan, the two Ruebens and I take the space and time capsule and hop to Earth-Z." He paused. "Everyone following?"

They nodded.

"Then I get out and collect a sample of the super-mutated time virus. With it being a time virus, I can only imagine how it has evolved since destroying the world. Anyway, then the three of us will warp backward in time on Earth-Z to around the tanker mission to search for the virus's Ground Zero when Rueben-Z was probably first infected."

"Talk about finding a needle in a haystack," Marshall remarked.

Aki turned to Rueben-Z. "You really don't remember anything about the tanker mission that was out of the ordinary?"

Rueben-Z shook his head. "I don't even remember finding that metal box in the control room like in the nanobot footage you showed me."

"That," Buzz said, "is why I think you were infected three to ten days before that. I now hypothesize that the messed-up nanobot footage is because the time virus was already in your blood. That's when it was starting to take hold and thus inter-fering with the nanobot."

Rueben shrugged. It was possible, but in his opinion, the tanker was the key to this as it was the first blank spot in the nanobot footage. However, there was no talking Buzz down when he was fully committed to a course of action. Besides, without Buzz, they wouldn't have a functioning space and time capsule.

Buzz continued. "Once I collect a sample of the virus from Ground Zero, we will all return to this Earth, and I should be able to unravel its evolutionary track so that we can eradicate it from the multiverse."

"You make it sound so easy," Rueben joked.

Marshall stood then and turned to face everyone. "I don't think that's funny." He glanced Rueben-Z's way. "How about we address the elephant in the room. How do we know we can trust this man? After all he's done."

Martha nodded in agreement.

Carolyn started to stand up for Rueben-Z, but he unfolded his arms and pushed off from the wall. He took a step toward Marshall and set his feet. "Mother, I can fight my own battles."

"You want to fight, son?" Marshall said.

Rueben-Z drew a deep breath. "Wouldn't be much of a fight."

Now Rueben jumped up. "No need to fight. We're on the same side now."

Marshall cocked an eyebrow. "Are we?"

Rueben-Z drew another calming breath. "I'll admit, I deserve the mistrust. There is no way you can trust me for sure. You'll have to take a leap of faith. I want to eradicate this time disease and fix all the worlds the same as you. I'm not the monster you think—hell, maybe I am a monster. I carry a world-ending virus in my veins. But look, sometimes you need a monster on your side to win the war." Rueben-Z finished by drawing another deep breath.

Marshall looked like he was trying to think of something to say, but then he dropped it. "You going to start meditating now? Sheesh. We oughta start calling you Rueben-*Zen*."

Martha stood then. "I don't think we have to trust you to work with you. I'm not sure you can ever make up for your actions. But...if everyone else is in favor of the plan, I'll go along with it too."

There was a tense pause. Then the tension started to ease as everyone nodded.

Buzz wiped the back of his hand across his forehead. "Whew. Well, now that we've cleared the air on that issue, there's only one problem with the plan."

"What's that?" Aki said.

"I don't know how to pilot the space and time capsule to Earth-Z."

Rueben-Z nodded. "Leave that to me."

"Right," Marshall said sarcastically.

Rueben-Z ignored him. "If you mirrored the capsule's software off the one in my old capsule, I can get us there."

"I did. Exactly," Buzz said.

Martha shook her head. "I don't like this. We're going to hand the keys to a time machine to a rogue time warper who we stole his warping powers from and who has already destroyed countless worlds?"

"Well," Buzz said, "when you put it that way..."

Rueben spoke up. "Buzz and I will be with him the whole time. Watching him. He won't be able to try anything funny."

"Why does he even have to go?" Marshall said. "If you ask me, I don't think we need him. We could keep him locked up here, so he can't hurt anyone else..." He let his words drop as Rueben-Z started to growl deep in his throat.

"Let's all calm down," Carolyn said. "Please."

Rueben-Z shook his head. "I get your animosity toward me. But you do need me."

"Why?" Martha asked.

"The dust."

"The dust?" some of them muttered in unison.

Rueben-Z nodded. "The last time I went back, the time virus had mutated. It blows across the world like a giant sandstorm. If you're going to take a sample, you'll need me there to guide you to safe coordinates. And to watch your back."

"Shit. Dust storms...I never thought about that."

Rueben joked, "How bad could it really be? We're going to Earth-Z, not that planet from *Dune*."

Buzz considered. "No, Rueben-Z makes a good point. There are a lot of living organisms on Earth, and on Earth-Z they'll all be dust now. And with unpredictable weather patterns. A dust storm could damage the space and time capsule, stranding us there. Or it could separate us like a fog..." Then his eyes twinkled. "Rueben-Z can guide us through the storm, but I have a solution to the getting separated possibility."

Buzz summoned Rosa, who brought him two tiny microchips. "I'm going to insert these into the two Ruebens—"

"Buzz," Rueben said, "we're not pets. Can't we just put them in our pockets or something?"

With a sigh, Buzz relented. "Yes, fine." He pulled up a program on his smartphone, which showed two beeping dots, one for each Rueben. "If we get separated by the dust, I can still find you both. Or, if Rueben-Z tries to make a break for it—"

Rueben-Z threw his arms up in the air. "Why would I make a break for it on a world I destroyed with no way for me to warp back and fix it?"

"Because we don't trust you," Marshall said. "Fine. If we all think this is the best plan, I'll sign off on it." A few moments later, Martha did too.

Buzz handed the two tracker microchips to the two Ruebens.

"Why does mine smell like goat?" Rueben asked.

Buzz snickered. "Because I had these tracker chips hidden in the collars of my goat and monkey that I kept at my mansion."

"Why did you put them there?" Martha asked. "Those animals weren't going to escape."

Aki glanced at her. "It was a big mansion…"

Buzz scoffed. "The tracking chips weren't for the animals. They were only a hiding place. These chips are very top of the line. Who would ever think to look for them in the collar of a goat and a monkey?"

He had them there.

"I have a question," Carolyn said. "What if you and the Ruebens run into big trouble back in the past on Earth-Z when you're searching for the virus's Ground Zero? How are you going to contact us here back on Earth-A?"

"A good question." Buzz straightened. "And one I have anticipated. Rueben and Aki told me about their encounter at the *Paper Warriors* newspaper place in Brooklyn…"

"I know it," Carolyn said. "But what's it have to do with—"

Rueben's eyes lit up. "The printing press. All those knobs and time stamps."

"Exactly." Buzz grinned. "I called them up yesterday to inquire about that printing press. I believe *Paper Warriors* exists on all the parallel worlds. Furthermore, I believe that it is possible to send a paper—or any printed message—from any of the worlds to the rest of the worlds." He chuckled.

"Those three poor fools running the place don't even know what it really does."

"You mean the three stooges?" Aki asked, and Rueben laughed, although no one else understood the joke.

Buzz continued. "If we run into trouble, or even if we want to send an update to those of us back on this Earth, we'll go to the *Paper Warriors* on Earth-Z and print a paper to this Earth at this exact date and time. You should be able to adjust the controls and time stamp to send a message back to us, based on the date and time stamp that is on our message."

"Who do we want to go there and wait for messages?" Aki asked.

After a few moments, Carolyn raised her hand. "I think I should. I'm the most familiar with the paper. Plus, I think it would be cathartic for me after their paper put Thorne on my trail."

Marshall reached out and touched her hand. "I'll go with her."

"Perfect," Buzz said. "Aki and Martha will stay here and hold down the fort."

The two women seemed all right with that.

Rueben turned to Buzz. "When do you want to do this?"

Buzz rubbed his hands together. "How about tomorrow morning? Maybe Carolyn can bake us another batch of chocolate chip cookies for good luck before we leave. If all goes according to plan, it shouldn't take us long to grab the two samples. At least, on this world, only a few minutes should pass. We have a space and time capsule at our disposal, remember?"

Rueben sighed. "Again, Buzz, you make things sound so easy."

CHAPTER TWENTY-EIGHT

Sunday, May 28, 6:45 a.m.

Rueben took another bite from his cookie. He was sitting next to Rueben-Z at the breakfast table. Everyone else was congregated in the kitchen, chatting and complimenting Carolyn on the cookies.

"Something's on your mind."

Rueben glanced up at Rueben-Z. "What do you mean?"

Rueben-Z smirked. "I was once your age. I know that look on your face."

Rueben nodded. He still found it strange that the parallel version of himself he was talking to was so calm and reasonable instead of furious and psychotic, the way he'd known him back when the virus was messing with the man's head. Carolyn and Buzz had been right when they'd said that switching the virus back to dormant would ease his psychotic tendencies. "You and Aki-Z. She really does mean the world to you, doesn't she?"

Rueben-Z washed down his cookie with a glass of milk. "She does."

"She's why you're doing this, right? I mean, you want to save everyone on all those worlds, but it's her you really want to be with again."

"I've been so lonely and messed up inside." Rueben-Z sighed. "If I can just see her face one more time, I'd be content. To look into her eyes, to hold her and my kids again without the virus taking them away again…"

Rueben glanced across the room at Aki chatting with Carolyn. She saw him and smiled. He smiled back. Then he turned to Rueben-Z. "That's why I trust you to go with us. Look, I probably shouldn't tell you this, but I talked with Buzz, and he said there's a way to reverse the warping cap we placed on you. Once this virus is gone."

"I appreciate that," Rueben-Z said. He ate another cookie and cocked his head at Rueben. "There's something else on your mind?"

"Yeah. You let your wife name your kid Montauk?"

They both chuckled, and Rueben-Z said, "It is a good movie though."

Rueben agreed.

Buzz informed Rueben that the space and time capsule would be ready to go in an hour. Rueben went first to find his parents.

He found them in the billiards room, talking softly to each other as they leaned against the pool table. Words couldn't express how glad he was that the two of them were back together. Part of him felt bad for interrupting their conversation.

"Buzz says we'll be leaving soon."

Marshall and Carolyn rose and stepped toward him.

"Be careful." Carolyn embraced him. "I love you, son."

"Love you too, Mom." Rueben pulled himself back and turned to Marshall, wondering how he would react.

At first, Marshall stood with his hands in his pockets. Then he came forward too and threw his arms around Rueben. "I'm proud of you. So damn proud." He mumbled something as Rueben pulled back.

"What was that?"

"Love you, son," Marshall mumbled again.

Rueben smiled. "Love you both too. And I'm happy for you."

Rueben was about to leave when Marshall chimed in, "You better come back in one piece. 'Cause you need to lock that down, what you got with Aki. Can't wait around with that one."

"Thanks, I guess?"

"Yep." Marshall made a dismissive gesture. "Now get out of here before the world explodes or whatever."

Rueben laughed and left to find Aki. On the way, he ran into Martha.

"Rueben, be safe."

"I will."

Martha looked like she wanted to say more. Suddenly she leaned forward and hugged him. "You're a great friend. Thanks for letting me in on this crazy, new part of your life."

Rueben nodded.

"I totally approve of Aki. You two will be very happy together."

He found Aki in the bunk room. She saw him and greeted him with a smile. He sat on the bunk beside her. They didn't say anything, and Aki leaned her head against his shoulder.

Rueben spoke up. "I know Buzz laid everything out nice and easy. But this mission is more dangerous than anything we've ever done. There's a possibility we may never come back."

"Don't even joke about that."

"Well, it's either that or cry like a baby—"

Aki smacked him playfully on the arm. "Rueben Peet, you're such a dork." She brushed the hair out of her eyes and laid a hand on his shoulder. "You're coming back."

"Yep, that's the plan…" He felt the warmth of her hand through his shirt.

She stared into his eyes. "You're coming back," she said again softly, pulling herself toward him.

He pulled her tight against him. "I love you."

"I love you too." She kissed him long and hard, and then they made love.

The time had finally come. Rueben, Buzz, and Rueben-Z had strapped into the seats of the space and time capsule. The door—which was more like a glass lid—*clicked* shut and Rueben stared out at his friends and family standing outside the glass.

Rueben-Z had already set the coordinates on the center console and was ready to make any last-second adjustments if necessary when they arrived on Earth-Z.

"You smell like sex," Rueben-Z remarked with an approving nod at Rueben.

"Guys, focus," Buzz said. "Ready?"

They were.

Buzz punched the button that activated the capsule.

Then they were gone.

When the space and time capsule stopped vibrating and was still, sunlight beat down through the capsule's glass lid.

"Moment of truth," Buzz said as he unlatched the lid. It rose to reveal the high rises of New York City. The time capsule was resting on the sidewalk. Cars sat jammed up for miles all around them, but there wasn't a single person in sight.

"Any way to confirm that this is Earth-Z?" Rueben asked. The buildings looked like the buildings he knew from Earth-A, but many of the cars looked sleeker, more futuristic-looking than he was used to. Was this what twenty years in the future looked like? New cars?

Suddenly, there was a loud rustling sound like the wind, and they all turned to see a massive cloud roll in front of the sun. Except it wasn't a cloud but a big veil of dust.

"This is Earth-Z, all right," Rueben-Z said as he climbed out of the capsule.

Rueben and Buzz unbuckled their harnesses and started to climb out too.

"I'd feel better with my body armor on," Rueben-Z muttered as he eyed the dust cloud.

"You're still on probation," Buzz said as he planted both feet on solid ground.

Rueben-Z was leaning up against the time capsule, still eyeing the dust. It was a good ways away but moving slowly, almost as if it was sentient and searching for something. "Really? I thought we were all good now. Rueben said you were working on a way to undo my warping cap."

Buzz flashed Rueben an irritated look.

Rueben patted himself off as he stood on the sidewalk. "Asshole," Rueben said to Rueben-Z. Rueben didn't like the serious look on the man's face. He looked like a mercenary sizing up the enemy.

Rueben-Z shrugged. "Takes one to know one." He started down the sidewalk toward a six-foot-tall telecommunications structure at the corner of an intersection.

"What the hell are you doing?" Buzz said as he fumbled the virus detector out of the capsule.

Rueben-Z didn't turn back. "Grab your sample kit and come on."

"We don't even know if the virus is present here," Rueben started to say. Then he saw the virus detector in Buzz's hands light up.

Rueben-Z stopped in front of the small structure. "Oh, it's here all right. Now hurry up before it spots us."

"Uh, Buzz," Rueben said, suddenly feeling a chill. "Do you feel that?"

A cool breeze whipped past them. The virus detector was going crazy. Buzz swallowed.

Thirty yards away from them, Rueben-Z kicked in the door of the telecommunication structure. It was about the size of a closet. He stepped inside.

"What is he doing?" Buzz asked as he pulled a glass vial from the capsule to take his virus sample.

Up in the sky, the giant dust cloud darkened and grew larger. There was now no mistaking that it had somehow detected them and was somehow coming for them.

Rueben-Z peered out from the structure. "Get over here! Now!"

Buzz closed the space and time capsule. Rueben grabbed Buzz by the arm, and they started for the structure.

When they reached it, they saw it was stocked full of guns, ammunition, and other weapons.

"What the fuck?" Buzz said. "How'd you know this was here?"

Rueben-Z smirked. "Because I'm the one who stashed all this stuff here. In case I had to come back."

Rueben's face tightened. "You knew that the virus had somehow…I don't know, gained sentience and would come after us if we came here? Why didn't you tell us?"

Rueben-Z scoffed. "Coming here is our best chance at finding a way to defeat the virus. I didn't know if it would've scared you from trying it or if you would've even believed me."

"Unbelievable," Rueben said. "I trusted you."

"Oh, don't be a whiner. We'll be fine. Here, take this." Rueben-Z thrust a pistol into Buzz's free hand. "Know how to use this?"

Buzz just stood there slack-jawed.

"Here. Stuff some of these in your pockets too." Rueben-Z tossed some grenades to Buzz.

Before Buzz could even protest, Rueben-Z was turning to Rueben with a semiautomatic rifle in his hands. "You know how to use one of these?"

"Yeah."

Rueben-Z handed it to Rueben. Then he gave him a few ammo magazines to slide into his pockets. "Better take some grenades too, this is probably gonna get ugly, and we can't afford to die now that we know that sucker feeds on time warping."

"We need to collect a sample…" Buzz said weakly.

Rueben-Z gave a shit-eating grin. "We can take a sample from that *thing* once we wound it. Come on, get with the program."

Rueben glanced out at the approaching dust cloud. It was only a block away now, and it had descended to street-level and taken on the form of a massive four-legged beast with giant hollow eye sockets and claws and teeth. It was so large it nearly took up the entire width of the street.

"You can't be serious," Rueben said.

"Sure wish I had my body armor on right about now." Rueben-Z strapped a submachine gun over both shoulders and selected a much larger, drum-fed machine gun for his hands. After stuffing his pockets with grenades, he turned to Rueben and Buzz.

"Oh well." Rueben-Z shrugged and test-sighted the gun. He growled, "You boys ready?"

BOOK 4 and the EPIC CONCLUSION TO THE DIE AGAIN SERIES WILL BE OUT IN FOUR WEEKS…

I hate camping.

There's a reason why we left the trees and I'm never going back.

I swore this the last time I went camping. It was my mantra, something I held true with every fibre of my being.

Back in 2003, I was living in Japan and I had the dumbest thought of my life. "I want to improve my Japanese (for all my efforts to learn the language – I can now find the bathroom in any restaurant in Japan. Yay, me!). I like camping (I was delusional). Why not combine the two? I know! I'll join a Japanese Camping Club."

Stupid Ramy! Stupid, stupid Ramy!

I joined the local university camping club and got exactly what I asked for. A camping trip.

To hell.

At the time I lived in Okinawa. Okinawa, I discovered as the club leader handed me chin and wrist guards, as well as a jacket that could resist the hardiest of zombie bites, is filled with all sorts of creepy crawlies that can kill you. Snakes, spiders, ticks ... the indigenous wildlife is downright dangerous.

As a result, we couldn't hike in the conventional sense. We needed to 'hike' in the river.

For 2 days, we swam. Well, I mostly floated as Akira – I shit you not, that was his name – dragged me in the water. Then for dinner we ate eel that we caught in the river (not bad) and canned dog food (I swear this is true). It was awful!

When we finally got home, I was so sore that I swore to everything I hold, held and will ever believe to be holy that I will never camp again.

Never!

Then I had kids.

And everything changed.

Don't get me wrong. I still hate camping. But I love my kids more.

And they wanted to go camping.

Damn me for procreating.

But then again – look at her face...

Thank you for not only reading this story but these author notes as well.

So, Ramy decided to eat dog food, walk on water, and swear. At least, that's how I took his story. Did *you* get that message from it?

(I humbly suggest my version made his reality 3x better.)

Back when I was old enough to drive, young enough to still be in high school, and stupid enough to want to stay up all night, I went searching for a solution to my addiction to sleep.

I needed it every night, like clockwork.

However, I was going camping with my cousins on my grandparent's ranch. Now, I had read all sorts of stories where real men stayed up all night.

So that was going to be me.

It was during the week before the big weekend, and I went looking for a solution to my sleep problem. I found myself in a local Houston grocery chain (Randall's) and did not have any ideas about what to do other than drink coffee.

Which I despised then and still despise today. Don't get me wrong, the smell is nice; the bitter flavor is gahh.

Not sure what to do, I asked an employee what I could do to help me stay awake. They suggested I go grab a product called "NoDoz."

At the time, I remember the box talking about how one pill was equivalent to two cups of coffee.

That should do the trick, right?

(I won't even get into the guilt where I thought I was purchasing a horrible drug. I solved my existential guilt issue by pointing out to myself I was buying it in a grocery store, not from a shady character on the street.)

I'll keep this short; I damn near killed myself. Or at least, it felt that way.

I had never had coffee, and I didn't do the math to realize that a cup of coffee was about 4x more powerful than a can of Coke. Which was what I normally drank.

So, we get up to the farm and go down to the tank. A tank is like a pond but manmade to hold water for the animals to drink. And to stock with fish for lots of fun.

My cousins and I grabbed branches, pushed logs into a circle, and basically became fire-nerds for an evening.

If a real animal had come upon us and growled, I probably would have wet my pants.

Anyway, sometime around 10:30-11:00 PM (my normal go-to-sleep time), I secretly opened the small bottle of NoDoz and took one.

Still feeling sleepy a couple of minutes later and NOT wanting to wuss out, I took another.

I'm now hopped up on 400mg (or about 20x the amount of caffeine in a can of Coke), and two things happened.

I got substantially sick to my stomach, and I was awake to feel every damned convulsion my body chose to dish out.

It was horrible.

Once I got the stomach pain under control, I started talking faster than an auctioneer trying to sell cattle.

For, like, an hour.

I finally wound down about 1:30 in the morning and decided that staying up all night was for idiots. I found a place to crash and laid down.

I swore to myself I'd never take NoDoz again for the rest of my life. Unlike Ramy, I've kept that promise, and I have never wavered.

I've drunk a LOT of Coke in the early mornings, though.

Ad Aeternitatem,

Michael Anderle

Other Middang3ard Books

Never Split The Party (01)
Late To the Party (02)
It's My Party (03)
Blue Hell And Alien Fire (04)

Death Of An Author: A Middang3ard Novella

Dark Gate Angels
Dark Gate Angels (01)
Shades of Death (02)
The Allies of Death (03)
The Deadliness of Light (04)

Dragon Approved
The First Human Rider (01)
Ascent to the Nest (02)
Defense of the Nest (03)

Nest Under Siege (04)
First Mission (05)
The Descent (06)
Sacrifices (07)
Love and Aliens (08)
An Alien Affair (09)
Dragons in Space (10)
The Beginning of the End (11)
Death of the Mind (12)
Boundless (13)

Other Books by Ramy Vance

Mortality Bites Series
Keep Evolving Series

CONNECT WITH THE AUTHORS

Connect with Ramy

Join Ramy's Newsletter

Join Ramy's FB Group: House of the GoneGod Damned!

Michael Anderle Social

Website: http://lmbpn.com

Email List: http://lmbpn.com/email/

Social Media:

https://www.facebook.com/LMBPNPublishing

https://twitter.com/MichaelAnderle

https://www.instagram.com/lmbpn_publishing/

https://www.bookbub.com/authors/michael-anderle